Silver Lining

Silver Lining

Silver Lining

Silver Lining

© Copyright 2021 Viola Tempest

Silver Lining

Cover Design by Ryn Katryn Digital Art

Table of Contents

Chapter One
The Creation of Silver Lining
12

Chapter Two
Dixon Reid
49

Chapter Three
Bethany Rose
77

Chapter Four
Date with Destiny
96

Chapter Five
Zoe Bryn
105

Table of Contents

Chapter Six
Blinded by Love
111

Chapter Seven
Thea
119

Chapter Eight
The Unexpected Truth
130

Chapter Nine
I Will Never Leave You
148

Chapter Ten
The Downfall of Society
156

Table of Contents

Chapter Eleven
Marissa Sinclair
166

Silver Lining

The Creation of Silver Lining

A treacherous gust of wind bent the branches of the old oak tree, just in view of the office window, and sent the pouring rain beating rhythmically against the office window. It created a tune that only Mother Nature could master.

Marissa Sinclair stared silently out the foggy window, wrapping her fox stole tighter against her shoulders, before sitting at the artfully arranged mahogany desk before her.

"One of these days, they really need to fix that air conditioner. I don't think I can take another day of this frigid cold," she whispered to herself, hugging her body closer.

All her belongings had a place—her pencils, her stack of papers, her folders, her stapler, everything.

Everything had a home, where it belonged. If anything was to shift out of place, she would know, even if she didn't see it right away. Her mind would continue to bite at her, unable to focus on anything else, until she figured out what was wrong.

Her OCD was always her biggest pet peeve. Only after everything got resorted back into their rightful places, could she actually focus on the bigger problems in her life.

Books, old and new, rested along the edge of her desk, stacked high to the ceiling, followed by piles upon piles of faxes and reports from her offices around the world. She leaned back against her rolling chair and stared at the two silver laptops in front of her.

The one on her left was opened to her stocks and finances while the one on her right was opened to her emails, currently fully organized. Thousands of emails, and not a single one left unread, even the ones that had trickled into her spam folder. Behind her laptops, hid her personal items.

Marissa always tried to keep her home life away from her work life, but spending so much time at the office often made her lonely, so she brought in some small reminders that she still had a life...sort of.

At work, she was ambitious, a somebody who had changed the world. It, at first, brought her awed looks.

Now, they were looks filled with fear and apprehension. There weren't all that many people left in her company, not the main offices anyway. Everyone used to be so eager to be a member of the company.

Now, no one would even step foot inside the building.

At home, her neighbors knew her as "the woman who never slept," always staring out her window as if she was waiting for an expected someone. They snuck silently around the hallways like they were thieves, avoiding her as much as possible, though she knew the glances they gave her when they thought she couldn't see them.

The lone recluse, only in a modern penthouse with all the best amenities instead of a broken-down hole. The one who made the world a worse place to be in, though why, no one knew. She was pretty sure she didn't know why either.

Her family hadn't spoken to her in years, and even if they did reach out, she had no idea what she would even say to them. What they would say back to her. She had isolated them all, chasing this dream for so long, that the only person she could rely on now was herself.

Worst of all, she felt no remorse or guilt.

She reached over and picked up a framed picture of her and her ex-fiancé, Levi Quinn. His arm thrown around her shoulders, smile firmly in place. She looked so comfortable in the hug, her eyes sparkling, though she'd never seen her own obvious happiness until she didn't have it anymore.

If she knew then the tragedy she knew now, she would have never gotten herself into that mess.

One of these days, she'll finally get her house. The house, the dog, everything. One of these days. But she doubted she'd ever get him back. It just seemed like a lost cause now.

Taped to the back of the frame was the note she had burned into her brain.

Babe, I love you, but I don't want you anymore.

Her eyes flew over the letters once again, remembering the way he twisted the tail of his y's. This was the eighth time she looked at it today since her morning had started.

She didn't know why she kept the picture, the note. She knew that holding onto the memory would only cause her more pain, leaving her incapacitated. But she couldn't find the strength to let go. She didn't want to let go.

What if? she thought. *What if?*

It hadn't been the most perfect relationship, but perfection didn't matter, not anymore anyway. Over the years, she realized it hadn't been all his fault.

He'd operated on the assumption that their relationship was only casual, and she assumed she'd be able to change him into something he wasn't and could never be. That he would finally stop looking at other women on his own, and that she would be enough for him, just as she was. That he would eventually love her if she'd kept waiting...and waiting...and waiting.

She'd played the role she knew would win him over, shifting herself into an opposing personality from who she really was, spontaneous, low maintenance, and a general go-with-the-flow type of girl, and then became angry that he took it at face value.

And when, finally, he found someone he wanted to make it work with, it wasn't her, after all she had done for him.

This was enough to send her over the patience threshold she had held in for so long. Because of this, she'd spent her time stalking him, staring at the photo of his wedding as her stomach churned. His new wife had that same happy smile Marissa used to have, but she was looser and more confident.

Marissa spent weeks comparing every little difference between them, trying to find what that woman had that she didn't, what she was that she wasn't. But, in the end, Marissa knew that was just a distraction from what she really wanted, a lover who understood her and loved her, just as she was.

Slowly rising from her chair, Marissa walked over to the display case opposite her desk and looked through the transparent glass at the tiny contact lens that was held delicately in place by numerous thin wires coming from the thrones under it.

The first prototype.

She creaked open the glass panel, picked it up by sticking it to her pointer finger, and looked at the inscription engraved on the thrones that held the lens in place.

Even in the darkest of times, a Silver Lining can always be found.

The tiny lens sitting on its throne stared up at her as she smiled back down at it, proud of her accomplishment. If she had known that everything in her life would change after she drew up the first draft, she would have put in a little more effort from the beginning. Done more tests, maybe. Something that wouldn't put her in the position she was in now.

Silver Lining was advertised as every lonely person's dream come true when it came to love, a lifesaver for anyone who had ever been dumped, cheated on, or crushed.

Silver Lining changed the world around her instantaneously, bringing happiness to the sad, and life back into the dead.

Marissa Sinclair was even known as the "Modern Matchmaker."

Those who were fitted with these lenses were promised a lifetime of true, loyal love and companionship, finally pulling them out of their screwed-up lives of heartbreak and meaningless sex.

No longer would people need to struggle to find a partner and love. No longer would people need to spend endless hours scrolling through dating apps in hopes of finding their soulmates. No longer would people endure heartbreak from their once-lovers leaving them for their best friends. No longer will rejection be a thing.

No, everything would finally be slotted in place.

Perfect.

Finally, people would be able to live happily ever after.

At least, that's what their marketing team promised. At the core of it, Silver Lining was just another piece of technology, and every technology came with its own share of inevitable flaws and mistakes. All they did was wrap it in some fancy words and gimmicks, and slapped a bow on top. But it worked. All too well.

Marissa walked back over to her desk and glanced at her laptop, smiling at the number. She was waiting for that number to finally reach a billion sales. She only had about a dozen left to go. And she did it. When she'd sold her millionth Silver Lining lens, her office was filled with happy and loyal colleagues as she popped open the champagne, the crowd bursting into cheer.

Her vice president at the time, Ian Cooper, had gotten her a giant flower arrangement and presented it to her amid cheers. She had been his hero at the time, looking up to her amicably as the successful person he strived to be.

That was before she sold control of the company to a random businessman, before she completely disregarded all she believed in and what she stood for. The other colleagues had all chipped in for a cake.

She could still remember the inscription, "To finding love." She wondered what they'd think of this now.

She thought she'd never stop laughing, never stop smiling, as everything had finally fallen into place. But that was just an ego boost, a temporary fix to her never-ending miserable life.

Back to reality.

Cooper left the position shortly after having his own lens installed and meeting his wife. She hadn't bothered to check up on him, but a piece of the flower arrangement stayed in between the pages of a book for years. She had no idea when she had forgotten the book's title; now, she couldn't find it even if she tried.

Now, she'd be lucky if she got a single congrats, or even a stare towards her that didn't have eyes filled with daggers. She slowly sat back down in her chair and leaned back, her right hand reaching over to refresh the page. A light smile grazed over her face as the numbers all evened out, and she finally reached her milestone.

A billion sales.

Who would have ever guessed that she would go from being broke to one of the most powerful entrepreneurs in the world?

She couldn't even count how many people hated her now. She started off so well, so loved by all her investors and customers, an icon. Now, all that remained was her legacy of screwing others over to get to the top.

She looked around her office, her bare and empty office with nothing but a dusty bookcase and a chandelier, held up her finger, and swirled it around in a circle. The office remained silent.

"Congratulations," she murmured into the empty room, then chuckled to herself.

Her wandering eyes soon landed on the lens again as she rolled her chair closer to her desk. She propped her head up on one hand and felt the smooth glass trace beneath the nail of her finger. It was the smaller model, like the lens in her own left eye, now turned off.

She had no idea if she would ever turn it on again. Maybe she should, just to torture herself as much as the lens' next victims. Why should she be free?

Her chest tightened as she studied it, remembering the years before and after Silver Lining had started…

* * *

The night was never-ending, and the flashing lights and thumping music made her far dizzier than the cocktail in her hand. The drinks were watered down, and the cover charge was high enough to make anyone wince.

Marissa leaned back against the wall and adjusted the bracelet on her arm. Red, signifying that she was a woman looking for a man, straight.

Champagne was the newest in a slew of sleek clubs catering to hookup culture, and definitely the swankiest. It was where the people went if they didn't want to leave alone at night.

The safety aspect appealed to people, while the exclusivity made them feel like they were above the regular masses, and soothed the egos that had been bruised from rejection.

If someone was here, there was a lower chance they would turn down going home with a complete stranger.

And sex, however meaningless, was better than nothing.

Before entering, Marissa picked a bracelet that indicated her sexual orientation, red, signifying that she swung with the opposite sex, and found out that there was a drink limit, but only on certain nights, probably the only reason she still had a brain intact. It was safe for when she needed an outlet, and the organization appealed to her senses.

Plus, she didn't have to spend the night staring at her projects or switching the channels on the television.

The inside of Champagne was like any other nightclub. A dancefloor took up most of the space, the interior was dark, and the lights were flashing enough to give her a seizure, a swath of beams in different neon colors washing over everyone in fast waves.

It was packed, like almost every night, but it was late enough in the night for the first wave of partners to have left.

Her eyes scanned the crowd, avoiding the men nervously shuffling in the corners, clearly their first time. The eyes of the eager ones would circle around like vultures, waiting for someone to make accidental eye contact to spark up a conversation, and the ones already out on the dance floor grinded up against crowds of young women without taking no for an answer. They weren't what she wanted.

Her gaze suddenly stopped at a tall man standing by the edge of the dance floor. His head was thrown back in laughter, and he seemed to be talking to everyone in the small crowd around him. He was definitely one of the more popular ones.

Marissa headed his way slowly at first, until she got close enough to see the red band around his wrist. That gave her courage, and she walked up to him with a smile.

"Hi, I'm Marissa."

She extended a hand. The thumping music meant she had to stand close to him if she wanted him to hear her. She could smell his delicious cologne despite the crowd of sweating bodies around him, but it didn't make her choke. He was handsome and sexy, but more than that, he was put together without looking out of place in the crowd.

"Name's Levi."

He caught her hand for a second. When he didn't pull her directly into him, or do anything borderline creepy in the first minute or so, the smile on her face became more genuine.

A drunk college student stumbled into him, laughing as she spilled her beer, so he gestured towards the nearest wall. Marissa nodded, and they moved away from the crowd.

Always a good sign.

"You have a nice smile."

Flirting to her was like going through a checklist. Smile, check. Twirl her finger into her hair, check. Look for signs of interest. The way his eyes panned down her body was one, the smirk that showed he was playing along, another.

Since the club didn't hide the reason why they were both there, they skipped over the awkward small talk she would normally engage in out in the public world. It really sped things up. She liked the efficiency.

It didn't mean she didn't find anything out about him though. She made a point to, just to be extra careful.

"So, you work in advertising? I'm assuming from the watch on your wrist, you have your own secretary."

"That's some good eye you have there. Smart, I like it. What about you?" Levi asked.

"Getting my Master's in computer science. It's been hell all week. I decided I needed to relax tonight, unwind, and just let go of all my stress," Marissa said.

"Maybe I can help with that." Levi winked and drew closer.

"I'm sure you can. My place, or yours?" Marissa bit her lip.

"Yours, definitely." Levi smirked.

The rest of the night was honestly a blur of sensation, a passionate affair she was so used to having.

It wasn't until the next morning, when she groggily raised her head from the pillow, to see him shrugging on his clothes and talking about the fact that he needed to go and pick up his girlfriend from the airport, that she realized this would probably never happen again.

Another one-night stand, just like them all. She had a vague recollection of him mentioning the girlfriend when they climbed up the stairs to her apartment.

"I'm assuming she knows about what, and who, you do at night?"

The shrug of his shoulders told her everything, but she didn't push. If she wanted to do this right, she needed to show him she was fine with it. That she would be a better choice, the one who would never push him into anything he wasn't comfortable with.

"You think you want to do this again sometimes?"

He turned around at that. "I already have one relationship. I don't think I can maintain another."

"Your relationship needs maintaining? Ouch. And no, I was thinking more about skipping the overpriced drinks and the cover charge by sending you a text next time I need to relax." She stretched out her naked body while she spoke, affecting nonchalance with all her being.

"Oh, that can be arranged." Levi drew nearer to the bed, gave her a fleeting kiss on the lips, and left.

Marissa honestly thought she was only after a steady semi-serious partner at first. A way to scratch an itch with a lot less effort. But as she got to know Levi more, the more she realized that he was everything she could ever want in a partner, as if someone had made him just for her.

She'd made a list once, a list no one had ever checked off until now. He was attractive, he made her feel desired, he was funny, and they had enough in common to hold a long conversation but not enough that they were exactly the same. He wasn't a loser, had a job he was passionate about, and he treated her like she had agency. He was just so…so…perfect.

She could be what he needed. It was the only way to get him to stay with her. To become his dream girl even when she wasn't. She wouldn't mind if he went out to be with other women, as long as she was the one he came home to.

The other one, Chloe, Marissa had found out her name after some careful probing, had only been with him for eight months, and she was already trying to change him, mold him into the perfect husband.

If she could show Levi that he'd be better off with her instead of that bitch, her life would be perfect. She just had to play her cards right. And she was good at that.

So, she dedicated her next three months carefully deconstructing Levi and Chloe's relationship, until that one glorious day when the words, "I broke up with Chloe," passed Levi's lips.

"Cool, means we have another apartment to pick from," was all Marissa could reply with without exposing her excitement too much.

She could tell he was surprised, how coy she was with the whole thing. It took another few months before he finally introduced her to people as his girlfriend. But that was okay.

She was finally good enough for someone to want her, to not run away after just one night. Even if it wasn't perfect.

Love never was.

* * *

Several years later, Marissa found herself sitting all alone in an empty apartment, staring at the clock ticking painfully slowly before her, and waiting for Levi's car to pull into the driveway. She wasn't worried that he had gone out, especially this late. It was the weekend, and she assured him that she would be completely fine with it.

He had been out with his friends late at least once every week since they had been together and came back in the wee hours of the morning.

No, that wasn't it. It was the fact that he hadn't even sent her a single message despite the several she had sent him that was the problem. It ate at her, the fact that he didn't even deem her worthy enough to tell her where he was anymore.

That's all she had ever asked of him, just a quick message letting her know that everything was okay before shutting her out for the rest of the night. Even a pocket-dial would have been better than silence.

She dropped her phone on the coffee table and walked away from it, swearing not to check it for at least the next hour. She made it to the bedroom door before she turned back to pick it up.

Nothing.

She went into the kitchen, grabbed a bottle of water, and downed the entire thing at once, trying to keep her mind and anxious assumptions from spiraling. She went back and checked the phone again.

Nothing. There was nothing. No unread notices at the bottom of her screen where the message icon was. No missed phone calls at the top of her screen where the phone icon was.

Nothing.

Desperate, she decided to check her email. It was dumb and probably too sad, but maybe the alcohol had fucked with his head so much that he had mistaken his email icon for his text. It didn't matter that he'd never done that before in the almost four years she'd known him. She hated herself for being so obsessed, for not trusting him, or worse, for thinking that he had died.

But she couldn't help herself.

When her email came up empty, she sat down heavily on the couch and began counting the fibers on the dark purple living room carpet. Usually, the rhythmic counting soothed her anxiety. It didn't work; she stopped every few hundred fibers to check her phone, trying her darndest to postpone yet another check for as long as possible. Her record was 15 minutes.

Ever since she'd been a young child, she always had this strange obsession with numbers. Her psychiatrist liked to brand it as Obsessive-Compulsive Disorder, but Marissa never called herself that. She didn't believe in branding people based on their personality and behavior.

Labels were just labels; they didn't mean anything more than simple name tags. Labels couldn't take away the uniqueness that people had and clump them into one category.

So, what if she did lay out her cereal flakes one by one and counted them before eating her breakfast every morning for the past ten years? So, what if she did count the mini square tiles on her bathroom floor every night before she could take a shower? So, what if she did run her tongue across her teeth to count them while driving to and from work, making sure they were all there before she could relax?

All that didn't make her any less normal than those who talked to themselves, or those who avoided stepping on the cracks of the sidewalk. Quirks didn't wreck society. And others had a lot more damaging ones than her. All she sacrificed to hers was time, something she had plenty of. And they calmed her when nothing else did.

She used to hide them, afraid that no one would like her or come near her if they knew her secret, but that only made them worse.

She tried to focus on something other than her phone, anything. She wished she could sleep through this agony like some people could, knock herself out and not endure any more of this torture, but she couldn't.

Instead, she moved through the apartment in a frenzy. She cleaned the kitchen completely, scrubbing at the tiles she just cleaned yesterday, getting rid of imaginary stains in the grout. She removed all her books off the shelves, dusted them from head to toe, and reordered them first by category, and then by color, before going back to category.

She even tried to count every strand of hair on her head, using a mirror for the back, and hanging a towel off the shower curtain rod so she could see it better in the shitty bright light.

It distracted her for a few hours, but nothing was enough. She even considered counting the specks of flakes that took up residence on her skin. She should have known that this was inevitable, chasing after a man she knew couldn't remain loyal. After all, she had granted it.

But after all that trouble she had spent getting him, she thought he'd be at least somewhat grateful and offer her the same respect in return.

Man, was she wrong.

The hours soon crawled to a stop. Marissa finally went into the bedroom, grabbed a book she needed to finish for one of her classes, and tried to focus on it, tuning out everything else. She took a red pen and religiously fixed every typo she found in the text. That helped keep her attention. It always worked in keeping her grounded whenever her anxiety flared up.

The thing was, she couldn't necessarily blame Levi for his behavior; they both lived different lives with different morals and ideals. And she accepted that long ago. This wasn't the first time this had happened, and it wouldn't be the last. They would argue, he would freeze her out, they would split, rage, and then fall back together again just as easily, a truly explosive relationship.

All because she was too afraid of being alone to not grant his every wish, and he found the perfect girl in her, someone who worshipped him while giving him the freedom to do whatever he wanted, including sleep with other women.

She wished she had the willpower to call the next time the final time, to see if her standing firm would make him change his ways, be devoted to her, just her. Even after four years, they were never the most stable couple; something always came between them.

Sometimes, she wondered how they agreed to move in with each other. They had broken up so many times that she was sure he'd lost count. She had to just give up trying to repair something that was destined to end in disaster.

She just needed to curb her loneliness for the time being, accept that Levi was the best she could do. She tried to ignore the voice in her head telling her that Levi was the only decent man who would have her, and that she needed to keep him, but it was just so convincing.

After all these years, she wanted stability. She deserved stability. Although she had all the time left in her life, she was running out of years to start a family, and while Levi had proposed the last time he'd reached out after an argument, she was too jaded to believe that marriage would change anything between them. And a baby would only make things worse. He'd just run off and leave her to deal with even more stress alone.

That never worked anyway. She knew far too many kids who were the result of that type of impulsive decision, and she could never put an innocent human being through that, no matter how easy it would be to pull it off when it came to Levi.

She dropped her book and leaned her head back against the pillow. She pressed her fingers into her eyes and groaned. Of all the men, of all the eligible bachelors in the world, why was she the unlucky one stuck with a man who cared more about pussy than he did about love?

Based on the conversations she had with Levi, it didn't seem like he was even capable of something as complicated as love. She didn't even think he knew what love was.

Yet, did she?

She'd once believed that if she just accepted his polygamous behavior as a part of him, he would get bored of it eventually and repay her for sticking around with devotion. She wanted to smack that version of herself now, nothing but foolish and naïve thoughts.

She heard the front door open and left the book she had barely read on the bed. She rushed out to the living room to find him kicking off his shoes toward the corner in the hall, smacking against the wall.

"Ah, good to be home." Levi sighed as he threw his jacket in the direction of the coat rack.

He missed, which meant he was drunk, but he wasn't staggering, and his eyes were not glassy, which meant he wasn't too out of it to not remember the conversation tomorrow.

Marissa's eyes widened. She could feel the words fighting to spill out of her, and she made a half-hearted effort to not blow up at him right then and there. She walked over to his face and stared straight into his eyes. He smirked at her.

"Where the hell were you?"

It burst out of her at a volume that would trigger their neighbors to file another complaint, especially since the sun had barely peaked over the horizon. She didn't want to start another fight, especially not after the brutal one they had two nights ago.

But his smirk made it difficult to control herself. The devious smirk that meant he won. Not if she had anything to say about it.

"Just a work thing, you know how it is." Levi walked into the kitchen and grabbed a can of beer. He turned to face her with a smile. "Why? What's up? Did something happen?" He popped open the can and took a sip.

"Did something happen? *Did something happen?* What do you mean, 'did something happen?' You know what I mean. Where the hell were you after work? It's four in the fucking morning, and you wreak of urine and semen! The least you could have done was send a text letting me know that you weren't dead and lying in a ditch! But no! I get nothing!"

"Is that supposed to be a joke?" Levi asked sarcastically as he tipped the can back and took another sip, relaxation evident in every line of his body.

It made her deflate.

"Fuck it. I'm going to bed. Dinner's in the fridge if you want it, but I'm sure the cum dripping down your chin was more than enough to fill you," she turned around and stomped to the bedroom.

Levi cut her off and grabbed her upper arm with his left hand. She turned towards him, and he frowned,

"Look, I thought I texted you. My phone must have died. I'm sorry."

His words emphasized regret, but Marissa knew better. This wasn't her first trial run. Levi was incapable of feeling remorse; he just went through the motions he knew would get him what he wanted.

His entire life, he had never been put in a situation where he had to feel shame or regret. During the times when he couldn't charm his way out of a problem, he was already halfway to Mexico by the time he needed to face the consequences.

"I know, Levi, I know, but sorry isn't enough." Marissa sighed and left.

She still hadn't recovered from their fight the night before, and she definitely wasn't in the mood for the cops to show up at their front door yet again. One more disturbance, and she was sure they'd take her away.

It took some painstaking tries, but she finally realized that contempt was a much better tactic than arguing. And it took much less effort. And she was so tired. She just didn't care anymore. She couldn't care anymore. She didn't have the strength to deal with his bullshit anymore.

* * *

Several hours later, morning arrived. Marissa found herself waking up alone, the other side of the bed still cold. She missed having someone to hold her and someone to hold back. She brushed her teeth and walked out into the living room, fully expecting to find Levi passed out on the couch like he always did after five too many drinks.

She tossed and turned all night, deciding to wait until the morning to apologize, after her nerves had calmed. She didn't want to do anything to jeopardize losing Levi, especially not after the last time he walked out on her.

But the living room was empty. The walls had been stripped of his posters, and all the drawers stood pulled open, as if gazing at the mess. In the kitchen, silverware, plates, and several picture frames of the two of them together were scattered all over the floor.

For a crazy moment, she thought they had been robbed, but she then noticed the things actually missing. The shelves that only held her things hadn't even been touched.

Levi was gone.

That realization slammed into her and, suddenly, Marissa couldn't breathe. She had to fix this; she couldn't be alone, not again.

Why did she get so upset at him? Why couldn't she just let it go and enjoy their night together like she planned? She was ready to surprise him with a magical night of a candlelit dinner and intimacy, but that all seemed meaningless now.

She ran back into the bedroom and grabbed her fully charged phone. Levi's number was on speed dial. She listened to the phone ring. And ring. And ring. She cursed and began pacing until the call timed out, and she got his answering machine.

"No, no, no, no, no," she cried as she tried to call again, only to go straight to his voicemail once again.

Devasted, she stumbled into the kitchen to pour herself a glass of chilled Sangria, when she came across a scrap of paper with letters scrawled over it taped to the fridge. At first, she quickly looked past it, assuming it was just one of her weekly grocery lists she had forgotten to take down. But as soon as she opened the door and reached in, her head popped straight back out.

No, it couldn't be just another list. Never in her entire life did she or would she ever not throw away something that was no longer of relevance to her.

She peered closer towards the letters and saw that it was a note from Levi: *Babe, I love you, but I don't want you anymore.*

Letting out a loud scream, she threw her phone against the wall and flopped down onto the couch. After several moments of staring up at the ceiling, she let out a sigh, curling up around a throw pillow, and burrowing her face in it, releasing another scream. She let the tears go.

But she wasn't surprised. Sure, she was devastated, but she wasn't surprised as this had happened before, many times. She always had unfortunate luck when it came to men, and she didn't expect that to change any time soon.

* * *

A few weeks went by, and Marissa still found herself alone in the apartment. She called in sick to work, started failing her classes, and spent her days sitting in the half-empty living room, staring blankly at the wall.

Levi had walked out on her before, but this was the first time he'd been gone for this long. Usually, he'd be back in a few days, or at least picked up the phone so she could apologize. But no matter how much she called or texted, he didn't answer.

She was pretty sure he'd changed his number, or blocked her; she didn't know which was worse.

After two weeks, she stopped expecting him to come back. And then, three weeks later, her phone rang. It was him, asking her out to lunch.

He'd cheated, she found out, seconds after the waiter poured them their glasses of water.

Not cheated as in he slept with a random woman as part of his one-night stands; she could handle that. Those were nothing new. Hell, she'd even encouraged that at the beginning of their relationship, wanting to not meet the same fate as most of his exes, then reluctantly accepted it as a fact of life. They had been through that before, and it hadn't come even close to breaking them.

She honestly didn't care if he slept around, if he slept with ten different women in one night, but he hadn't. He had been in a serious relationship with someone else, spending his nights with her instead of with Marissa, and even going as far as proposing to her. Apparently, it wasn't monogamy that Levi couldn't stand. It was her.

"I just don't think we work anymore. I don't think we've ever worked, honestly. Most nights, I just saw you as another body to keep me warm. We just hurt each other more and more, and we both deserve better than that." Levi sounded reasonable, hands around the coffee cup on the table.

His face was passive, open, like he didn't notice he'd just ripped her heart out, and she was struggling to breathe.

"Better? Better than what?" She knew she sounded hysterical.

"I can't give you what you want," he said, his tone harsh.

"But you can give it to her," Marissa spat out.

"It's easier with her. She doesn't think I'm something I'm not nor does she expect me to be," Levi said.

"I've always accepted you. I broke my heart trying to accept you."

She wanted to throw her coffee in his face. It was cold enough to not scald him.

"That was the problem. Everything we had together was fake because you just molded yourself into whoever you thought I wanted you to be. You accepted that I had unhealthy coping mechanisms." Levi raised his voice, then lowered it when the other people in the coffee shop turned around. "Other than that, you just shoved me in a box and assumed I'd fill it. For fucks sake, we met in a sex club and haven't had a meaningful conversation in the four years we'd been together. What did you know about me before you decided we'd be good for each other? Before you suddenly decided that we were soulmates. Or did you just go through a list and say, 'Good enough?' Hell, how much do *I* even know about *you*? Did you ever tell me who you really are, or did you create a persona I could see myself with and play off of that? Anything personal I know about you, I know because you couldn't hide it from me. That is not a relationship, Marissa."

"So, now what, you replace me with some slut and, suddenly, you're all better?" Marissa asked.

"No, but I'll try and not fuck it up this time around. I only stayed with you for this long until I could make a clean break from you," Levi said.

It was those last words that did it. She threw her coffee in his face, making him sputter, and left. Hypocrite. She wanted to scream so many things at him. That sex wasn't the only way to cheat, that a clean break wasn't him leaving in the middle of the night. But it wasn't like it would do anything to help.

So, she gave up. She began to think love wasn't really for her after all.

Work helped her focus. She didn't have to spend her days in the empty apartment. At night, it became too hard to stay in said apartment, all the loneliness creeping up on her.

But she could stay somewhere else. There were enough dating apps and online hookups to make sure she didn't spend any time reflecting on her shitty situation. Plus, there were a lot of willing men to help her try and forget.

But every rejection, and every date gone wrong, made the thought of being alone forever float through her mind. When she had Levi, she felt a sense of security, a home she felt like she belonged in, despite their relationship being volatile.

Now, she found herself on a sinking ship, unable to grab hold of a hand to safety.

She kept going on dates, one or two a day, trying to find a distraction. She couldn't step foot in a nightclub without thinking of Levi, but there was nothing stopping her from going to dinner and out for coffee. And she could keep getting disappointed.

There was Chase, who thought the ideal way to get in her pants was to talk about how much money he earned, tell her she was not like other women because she was actually smart, and imply that the dinner he bought her meant she had to sleep with him. And, of course, those men were the ones who were the worst in bed. Definitely nothing to brag about.

In fact, that last point seemed to be something a lot of the men had in common. Like Matt, who acted insulted when she asked to split the bill, expecting her to foot the entire thing because she was the only one who actually had a job out of the two. That's the last time she'd date a gamer.

Then there was Luke, who seemed nice, approachable, and someone she could really see herself with, even though he sounded a bit too safe and dependable after the rush she had gotten from Levi's antics. Until she saw him with his very pregnant wife in a grocery store one weekend.

Were there any decent men out there anymore?

She wasn't even counting the men whom she had to block right away out of fear and disgust, or the guys who stared at her chest instead of her face, or the ones who obviously sent the same message to every freaking woman out there, some even forgetting to take her off group chats when they did so.

In the end, she had to ask herself if she ever had a decent relationship with a man, any man. Thinking back to the three relationships before Levi made her feel dirty, so that was a no. They were all the same, the next one worse than the first.

The first one was the high school sweetheart who dumped her when she "got too difficult to handle, even with the great sex." His exact words. The one who just wanted a homemaker, and the one who stated she was crazy and actually made her OCD worse the longer she stayed with him. It was the only time she had ever been hospitalized.

Bars were a bust too. Marissa was average looking, nothing flashy, but she could pick up most men for the night. But only for the night. They all seemed to leave before the sun could even rise. She knew how to flirt, how to catch men's attention, but everything after that was a tragedy.

She had no idea how to keep a relationship, turning men away by date number two. Though, it seemed no one did.

After all her failed attempts, and the sickening feeling in her stomach from her desperate efforts to force love her way, she decided to look more closely at the matchmaking apps.

Not for herself; she had tried that route, all of them ending in a disaster. This time, to look at other people's results, to see whether it was just her with the shitty luck.

What a scam, she thought to herself, the more she looked into them.

Sure, there were tons of dating apps and dating websites, all claiming to help people find true love and their soulmates, but none of them ever seemed to work, the hundreds she had tried.

How were apps supposed to know people's "perfect partners" by asking only a few simple questions? Some didn't even ask any, just dumped photos on their desperate customers (real or fake), using marketing schemes to sell them with a "one true love" aspect.

The creators didn't know. Using an algorithm may have helped with finding commonality between what and who people preferred, but no way could it ever account for the vast differences between each individual human being.

Plus, everyone on these apps always lied, portraying a side of themselves that obviously was too good to be true, as she learned the hard way. No algorithm could ever find the "perfect match." All Marissa ever found through these hoaxes were perfect disasters, nothing she could bring home. They all seemed to have the promise of "forever," but as soon as she said that first, "I love you," they'd buzz away like bees.

There had to be a more efficient way of finding true love. She had always been good with numbers. So, she dove into the statistics. Some of these apps had their codes online, so she combed through them. She read up on sites and research. And eventually came to only one conclusion.

She could do better. She had to do better. She was determined to create that perfect app for true love.

Fed up with her lack of luck, she saw no harm in giving it a try. If nothing came out of it, at least it would be a good distraction for her for a few months while she got over Levi.

So, she scrapped her initial topic and gave herself a seven-month deadline. If she had nothing by then, she'd give up on love and settle for meaningless sex the rest of her life. The boys would be proud. She could even get a cat and complete the image.

Her research veered off track spectacularly after only one month. Everything she came up with was complete trash, nothing different from the hundreds of existing trash already out there. She needed to do better, come up with something "special." She didn't need an algorithm; she needed a way to connect the brain to the app itself. She needed an implant. She needed to study the brain.

Starting an entirely different field of study meant her previous deadline of seven months didn't work. She was lucky she had savings and a rent-controlled apartment, because, otherwise, she would have been left out on the street. Finding love was way more important than a job she hated, and if she could just pull this off, she'd never have to live in fear of being hurt ever again.

She just couldn't focus on anything else. Especially not after she realized she could do what she wanted with a single lens.

It wouldn't be an instant partner summoning. The lens would scan certain parts of the brain and deliver jolts that mimicked neurons firing, to make the brain see what wasn't there. The perfect person for anyone, based on preferences the person wearing the lens didn't even have to be aware of. She decided to call the people created by the lens, the Zetas.

Life with the Zetas would heal wounds from bad relationships, show the person wearing the lens what they truly deserve, offer companionship for people without scarring them. And people could always turn them off if they ever met a real person equivalent or needed a break. The off switch was the safety feature Marissa couldn't do without.

She needed some help getting the lens up and moving as this was just a prototype, but she believed she finally found the answer to falling in love. For months, she struggled with finding different ways to fuse the lens with the proper conductor so it would connect to the lobes of the brain, entering through the eye socket and linking to the temporal and occipital lobes of the brain, turning the user's eye to metallic silver when worn.

And she needed a way to test it. Since she wasn't going to up and ask someone to be her guinea pig, she decided the first prototype would be in her own eye. Taking out a loan to hire a surgeon to install the lens was stupid according to some, insane by others.

Hell, her family and friends thought she'd cracked, kept trying to take her to a doctor or lock her up in a straitjacket to stop her. Luckily, they didn't have a way to do that, not legally, anyway.

And once she did, she would be able to tell them what she had been working on. She could save everyone from heartache. She made sure the surgeon she hired was certified and went under the knife.

It was just a small change, a discomfort in her eye, but when she turned the lens on, her life changed forever. As soon as she left the doctor's office, she saw a man standing on the opposite street, sexier and more beautiful than any man she had ever laid eyes on. When she looked him in the eyes, he smiled.

Marissa pressed the button on the remote she gripped in her hand, and the man vanished. Success. She grinned, and took a side street, so people wouldn't see her talking to herself before she pressed the button again. Her mind made the guy follow her. She observed him.

He was tall but not too tall, well-built but not a bodybuilder, with dark hair and handsome dark eyes.

And though she knew he was just a Zeta, he seemed so real, like she could just reach out and touch him.

"Hi, I'm Marissa." She extended a hand at him.

"I'm Blaise. I saw you, and I couldn't help but say hi," he said.

She shivered at the French accent and smirked. The lens sure knew what she had fantasized about. She accepted an offer to go to the movies and couldn't remember the last time she had so much fun. He was the man she dreamt about her whole life, a man even more perfect than Levi was. Polite, dedicated, and he never even turned once to look at another woman.

To him, Marissa was the only girl in his eyes.

He was perfect, absolutely perfect.

* * *

Two years later, Marissa found herself standing in front of SENSA, the world's largest dating app conglomerate located in the heart of Boston, Massachusetts, twisting at her fingers and nervous to present what she thought was a life-changing invention, the next step in the future of love.

"Marissa, so glad to finally put a face to the voice. I'm Jackson, Jackson Matthews. We've been speaking on the phone for several days now." Jackson smiled as he extended his arm towards Marissa.

He was the only person out of hundreds in the industry who responded to her email. He was the type of man she would have gone for back in the day. He was tall, slim, with a good smile, and a professional demeanor. Now, it didn't really matter. She didn't need anyone else but Blaise.

Love was finally moving in the right direction for her.

Standing up from her chair in the lobby, Marissa returned the shake, her hand sweating from the tension that was her body beneath her pencil skirt.

"Nice...nice to meet you, Jackson. I'm glad we can finally meet in person."

"New to this market?" Jackson chuckled.

"How did you know?"

"I can tell. No need to be nervous. We've all been in your shoes. Hell, I'm still in your shoes. Some of us just don't have the best people skills either. Just minutes ago, I wiped my hands on my pants before coming out here."

"Yeah," Marissa whispered.

"Come on, let me take you back. Everyone's really excited to see this 'lens of love' as we like to call it."

The meeting room was intimidating, a row of suits staring at her from an expanse of glass and chrome. There were no walls, only windows, so the entire floor could see what was happening inside. If she humiliated herself, she would have to avoid this entire block for life.

Marissa set up her laptop in silence, acutely aware of the sweat working itself down her spine.

"Thank you for meeting with me today. My name is Ma...Marissa Sinclair." She cleared her throat and took a long sip of water before finding the nerves to continue. "We all want love; that's a basic human need that can't be ignored even if we tried. I, like many others, I'm sure, am tired of chasing after love, being in a relationship just to watch it fall apart, having to start over year after year.

Now, I know the solution to finding that 'perfect soulmate' used to be dating apps, given the chance to scroll through millions of eligible singles and narrowing down the right match. But although dating apps have been around for decades, how accurate are they, really?

Only three percent of people who meet their partners on dating apps actually end up together for life, the rest fizzling out with a couple one-night stands. Despite how good you think your algorithm is for finding love, it's flawed."

Marissa paused to hear the gasps and whispers around the room before continuing, "I want to present you all with what I think will provide guaranteed love, love destined for forever. Please turn your attention to my design, Silver Lining, a contact lens that is GUARANTEED to help users find their one, true love, the perfect match for all their needs.

No longer will we need to play Russian Roulette with our hearts. Let me explain how this works. When a person wears the lens, it will automatically connect to their brain and extract all the information about the person's desires and interests when it comes to the perfect love, all without that person ever lifting a finger.

Silver Lining will then computer generate the perfect specimen for the user, a virtual reality that feels so real to the person, like they have finally found their soulmate. These specimens, or Zetas, resemble humans in every way, from their physical appearances to their physical touches.

Never will users feel like they're not with a real person, the perfect match guaranteed to end loneliness and rejection. The best part is, Silver Lining is completely removable. Wear the lens to find your true love; take it out when you need a break. No commitments!" By the end of her speech, her nervousness was gone, replaced with butterflies in her stomach.

"How does it work?" one of the investors, Bella Dawson, asked.

"I'll spare you the boring science talk and explain it as plainly as I can. It scans certain areas of your brain, and then fires small electrical currents that mimic brain waves. The first action builds the computer-generated partner, a Zeta, while the second releases it. The client will feel like they are talking to a real person. All actions will feel real."

"How will that help people find their match?" Bella asked again, leaning forward with curiosity.

"Some people don't know what they want. Some people are too broken or monstrous to deal with actual people. Some just need companionship to get through their life at the moment, until they are ready. The lens can solve all of this. And when they are ready for a real-life commitment, they remove it. They could also keep it in, if they decide the relationship with the Zeta is all they need."

"How do you know it works?" another investor, Dean Warwick, asked, looking at Marissa with a raised eyebrow.

"I'm glad you ask." Marissa clicked on the laptop, and a file, along with a photo generated by her own lens, appeared on the big screen connected to her laptop. "Meet Blaise, my perfect match. 6'2", brunette, athletic, and the most gorgeous eyes you will ever see. He is everything I need plus more. Never a disappointment. Never a rejection, for it is impossible for him to leave. Complete loyalty. And he is truly happy to be with me. Trust me, I have faced rejections all my life. Blaise is my answer, my Silver Lining."

"You... have the lens installed?" Bella asked, stunned.

Marissa smiled and clicked the button on her bracelet. From the gasps, she knew her left eye had turned silver. She saw Blaise appear to her behind the investors, waving, proud of her. His dark hair was slick, and he wore clothes a bit too casual for the space they were in, but he was still gorgeous. She stifled a grin and turned the lens off.

She had more to say. "I have my second prototype. I also have a report from the doctor who did the installation, to ensure you of the lens' safety."

She let the slide show run, showing images from her own dates, taken from her point of view. She'd managed to find a way to show her own point of view to other people, plugging in a computer into the lens by tracking the signal emanating from the lens and the remote.

After one of the longest pauses she had ever experienced, Dean spoke up once again, "Thank you, Ms. Sinclair. We'll talk through this amongst ourselves and let you know. Jackson will show you out."

"Thank you. Thank you, everyone. I hope to hear from you soon," Marissa responded, fearing the worst.

As Jackson closed the door, she heard the room erupt in murmurs.

"Great job in there! I thought that was a fantastic presentation." Jackson beamed as he escorted Marissa to the elevator.

"I'm glad you thought so. I couldn't read any of their emotions," she whispered back.

"Nah, don't worry about those sticklers. You can't get a smile from them even if you brought in twenty puppies. I could tell though. You definitely intrigued them. I'm intrigued too. I know we've talked about the lens in detail already; that's why I was confident in calling this meeting, but I hadn't seen it in action."

"Well, I hope so. I really think Silver Lining is...."

Marissa's train of thought was distracted by the sound of her phone. She fumbled around for it in her pocket before finding it, answering the call and pressing it to her ear.

"Hello? Yes, this is Marissa. What? No way! Really? Oh my god, thank you! Thank you! I promise you won't regret this!" She hung up her phone and turned to Jackson. "I got it! They said 'yes!' I got it! I'm in!"

"See, I knew it. I told you they were interested. That's fucking awesome, Marissa. This is definitely a life-changing invention. You're going to change how everyone sees love forever!" Jackson leaned in for a congratulatory embrace, and Marissa hugged back.

After the excitement had died down, Jackson and Marissa still found their arms wrapped around each other, staring into each other's eyes with lust. While her mind was perfectly able to imagine Blaise kissing her, feeling another person against her was different.

More shocking. It brought back memories of her old ways, when she fantasized about every man who paid her the slightest of attention. Jackson leaned down to kiss her, inserting his tongue into her mouth. Marissa kissed back. For a minute, then pulled back.

"No, I can't. I'm with Blaise."

However, Jackson refused to take "no" for an answer. "Come on, Marissa. You and I both know that these Zetas, or whatever you're calling them, can never truly replace the touch of another human being, despite how real it feels," he responded as he pulled her in closer and kissed her again.

That relationship had been the nail in the coffin of Marissa's trust in actual men. They had a week-long whirlwind romance before she came up for air long enough to look him up online. Just to find an article about him marrying an heiress a year prior. Another liar, not like she expected anything different based on her past history.

Marissa didn't cry or scream or beg. She simply walked out of his hotel room, called the company, and cut Jackson out of the entire project in one fell swoop. No more crying. No more begging for love. No more. She was done. She hadn't even stayed to see his face when he got the notification.

* * *

The next day, she got a message from Jackson.

What the fuck, Marissa? I go to work only to be told I'm no longer working there? Why?

Marissa just sent him the link to the news article and turned off her phone. She then turned her lens back on.

"Breakfast in bed?" she heard Blaise knock on the door.

She had all she needed. No man in this world could ever replace Blaise. He was all she'd ever need. She would probably never turn him off again.

* * *

Marissa closed her laptop and stood up from her chair again. She had made a name for herself and changed the way people experienced love.

So, why wasn't she happy? Why wasn't she celebrating with the others instead of sitting in her office alone? Why had she turned off her lens tonight, so she could truly feel how alone she was?

She walked over to her door and grabbed the jacket hanging on the hook. She sighed and held it close to her chest. Even after all these years, she still kept Levi's favorite jacket. At first, she cherished it because it smelled like him, but now, she had no reason to wear it. But it just felt wrong to let it go.

Silver Lining

Carefully, she pulled the jacket over her shoulders, stuck her hands into the pockets, and headed home.

Chapter Two

Dixon Reid

Dixon Reid tapped his fingers nervously against the table as he waited for his girlfriend, Zoe Bryn, to arrive. She called minutes earlier to let him know that the subway had broken down in Midtown, and she was going to be a few minutes late.

NYC's subway system always malfunctioned, and Dixon cursed it every time he found himself sitting alone in a restaurant, like a pathetic soul who had been stood up once again.

But this wasn't the first time Zoe had run late. It had been such a pattern that Dixon lost track, blaming the wretched subway by default. Sure, he was curious at first, suspicious as to whether the subway really was to blame, but he trusted Zoe, and he knew first-hand how terrible those crowded trains could be.

Besides, he couldn't let his nerves ruin their night. Tonight, was the night. After four agonizing years of relationship drama, he was finally ready to settle down.

Sure, Zoe wasn't the woman of his dreams, but he was thirty-six, and if he wanted to start a family any time soon, he couldn't risk starting over, not again. Zoe had to be the one. She just had to. They had their issues, like all couples do, but once he showed her he was committed, he was sure that she would change, and they would be happy again.

He called ahead to Étoile, the hottest new French restaurant in town, weeks ahead, ensuring that they had the most expensive wine and handing them a list of songs he had written specifically for Zoe. Besides, that was how he was able to woo Zoe the night they met.

She was always his strongest supporter, even going out of her way to support him financially when he was just starting out in the music industry. He knew how rare that was, and even then, he had vowed to never take it for granted.

Now that his first and second album had both gone platinum, he could do whatever he wanted. And what he wanted to do was spoil her.

Not that Zoe was a gold digger. She still worked at the law firm she had been at when they'd first started dating, only now at a much higher position. He was pretty sure she was going to make partner one day, and he couldn't wait to celebrate that with her. And now, he could call her his wife instead of his girlfriend.

He had made it.

They had both made it, the ultimate power couple.

The night was going to be perfect, absolutely perfect. It had to be to fix the nightmare they had both been going through. The past few nights were pretty rough. Dixon and Zoe struggled to see eye-to-eye on nearly every conversation they had, leading to endless nights of arguments, from where they were going to go on vacation to the type of drain cleaner they needed, everything.

It was all getting to be too much.

However, tonight was going to change that. His romantic proposal would make her fall back in love with him again, and he would give her the wedding that every girl wished she could have. Everything was planned to the dot. From the string quartet, to the serenade, to the short amount of time he had reserved the restaurant for.

But she was running late. Again. Of all nights, she was running late.

Perfect.

Every anniversary they had in the past was always the same. On their first one, they'd promised each other to never be late for any of their anniversaries, the one promise they swore to each other they would keep no matter what. Dixon had always managed to keep his promise.

For the past three years, Zoe, on the other hand, always managed to blame the subway for her tardiness, sincerely apologizing, but Dixon could swear that during the third year, she showed up to dinner with her hair disheveled and her bra half-hooked. But he didn't mention it and let it go.

This year didn't get any better. He took the day off specially for this moment, but she didn't seem to care at all, not even a simple kiss on the cheek before rushing out the door early in the morning.

She couldn't even bother to text him back about her day or their dinner plan, only responding ten minutes before their scheduled reservation. Not even a follow up. He knew lawyers were busy, but it wasn't that hard to text someone back, especially since he knew she's always posting on her social media accounts.

He leaned back in his chair and held up a finger to get his waiter's attention.

"Another scotch, please," he said, offering him a smile.

"Right away, sir," the waiter threw back.

He snagged Dixon's empty glass from the table and headed towards the bar. Dixon imagined the man hid his laughter behind the mask of polite service. Who reserves an entire restaurant and then gets stood up? Especially a man who was as famous as Dixon was.

Dixon sighed softly and reached into his pocket again to pull out the small red velvet box. He flipped it open and examined the ring. It had belonged to his great grandmother before she died, a treasure that had been kept sacred in their family for generations.

"Hey, Dixon. Sorry I'm late," Zoe said, breathless, as she came up from behind him.

He snapped the box shut and dropped it back into his jacket as quickly as he could, then he looked up. Her hair was windswept, but other than that, she looked as normal as a woman who had rushed through the bustling streets of NYC could look. He stood up to pull out her chair for her and gave her a kiss, grazing her cheek as she turned away from his lips.

"It's fine." He chuckled softly. "The waiters have all been very kind and kept my glass full while I waited."

"Oh, perfect," she responded, obviously trying to keep her tone even. But her disappointment and anger shined through. "Guess I'll be driving us home tonight."

"I promise not to drink more than a glass of red wine for the rest of the night," he reassured her as he took his seat again. He stared across the table at her before shaking his head. "God, you look beautiful tonight."

"Thanks," she said, pushing her hair back. "I didn't even have time to get ready. I ran straight here from work. I don't even know how long it would have taken me if I had stopped at home first to get ready."

"Well, you look nice either way, darling," Dixon said with a wink. "I'm just glad you showed up at all."

She laughed and shook her head. "You think I would miss the chance at a free dinner?" she teased.

He took in a deep breath and calmed himself down before nodding. "Right. And the fact that it's our anniversary...did that cross your mind at all?"

She raised an eyebrow and looked over the menu at him. "Shit, is that today?" she asked.

"Yeah, it's today. I mentioned this to you just yesterday. I even took the time to mark it on your calendar," he told her, giving her an incredulous look. "Why do you think I took today off? How could you forget something so important, so meaningful, to our relationship?"

"Sheesh, calm down. We go out to dinner every Thursday," she retorted. "I didn't even realize what day it was, Dixon. I'm sorry. I would have bought a gift for you if I had remembered that it was today. I can't believe I didn't even realize what day it is."

"Oh my god," he muttered, shaking his head. "Unbelievable."

He picked up the menu and stared at the pages despite having ample time to look over it the entire time he was waiting for her.

"Well, like I said, I'm just glad you showed up, even if you didn't remember and didn't bring a present. I think you can make it up to me later."

They went silent while they both looked over the menu. However, Dixon was still stuck in his own head. Going around and around the fact that she had somehow forgotten their special day, the one day out of the year they had both sworn to each other they would always remember. He did everything he possibly could to remind her, and she still forgot. He couldn't believe it.

Did he really mean that little to her?

He was still upset by the time their food came, not even bothering to say a single word to her despite being so excited just minutes earlier. He couldn't find any words that weren't hurtful to say, and he didn't want to cause more of a scene.

Zoe sighed loudly, apparently having enough of the silent treatment.

"I already said I'm sorry, Dixon," she told him. "I don't think I need to say it again."

He paused in bringing the piece of steak to his mouth and glanced up at her. He let out a small sigh before setting his fork down. He grabbed his napkin and wiped his mouth before standing up.

"Oh, come on, don't be dramatic." She sighed, shaking her head. She turned to her food. "If you leave, I'm not running after you."

Dixon hesitated for a moment and gripped the lapel of his jacket. He shook his head and pulled out the ring anyway while getting down on one knee.

"I don't want to do this while angry so I'm going to let everything else go."

"Oh my god," she whispered, covering her mouth.

"I love you, Zoe Bryn," he told her, taking her other hand. "I love you more than I love anything in this world, and I want to spend every waking moment with you. I want to share a home with you, a life with you, and a family with you. Will you marry me?"

Tears started to roll down her cheeks, and she nodded quickly. She couldn't find her voice to say even a small, "Yes." She barely looked at the ring, too busy pulling him into a hug.

"I love you," he whispered as he hugged her back.

A few of the staff members clapped as the waiter came over with a large bottle of wine.

"The manager of Étoile wishes for you to have this," he told them after they pulled away. "Would you like a glass now, or would you like to take it home to save for later?"

Zoe looked at the bottle before looking at Dixon.

"We get to keep that?" she asked, moving to take the bottle from the waiter.

"Yes, ma'am." The server smiled, handing the bottle over. "It's one of the best wines we have at the restaurant."

"We'll take a glass right now," Dixon told him before moving to help Zoe back into her seat.

He leaned down and kissed her, holding it for a moment. When he pulled away, he went back to his seat, smiling like a proud and newly engaged man.

For the rest of dinner, he couldn't believe how incredibly lucky he was. He couldn't stop thinking about how he was going to spend the rest of his life with her, the future mother of his children.

* * *

During the first couple weeks after the proposal, Dixon couldn't wait to finally get married. They initially decided on a June wedding. Dixon really had his hopes on getting married in December under the falling snowflakes, but Zoe had been insistent on it taking place in the summer. She seemed excited to plan the wedding together, from tasting all the delicious cakes, to picking out all the beautiful flowers, to deciding on the band they wanted to hire.

Dixon even accompanied Zoe to Beauty & Bridal to try on wedding dresses. Zoe's mother tried to insist that he stay out of it, but Zoe wanted her fiancé to be part of her special moment. Their wedding was going to be their special day.

However, it didn't take long before Zoe began to grow distant again and express contempt towards Dixon. Pushing them back into the same downward spiral as before the engagement.

"Hey, Dixon, let's push the wedding date back a couple years. I think it would be better for us to wait until we're more ready, to see where things go," she told him, lightly touching his hand as they sat in the living room together one night while watching a movie. "We don't want to rush into anything."

Dixon frowned and looked down at all the magazines and pictures they collected to plan the wedding.

"A couple years? *A couple years?* What about all the deposits I put down? The cake alone cost eight hundred dollars! That's money we can't get back! And all the caterers? What about them? Why didn't you say something when we started planning everything? Why'd you wait until now? We already booked the band that you insisted on."

"I don't know. I'm just not really feeling it lately. I don't even know if I want that band anymore. I'm thinking maybe a DJ? You know my friend, Felix? He's a great Mixmaster. Maybe we can connect with him," she told him, grabbing her phone and sending a text before facing back towards him.

Dixon frowned and shook his head. "What's going on with you?" he asked. "We literally spent six weeks trying to plan everything, and now you want to push it off? Why? Do you not want to marry me anymore? I can't keep playing catch up with you and your indecisive mind. We've been together for four years. Four years! Do you want to be with me or not?"

"Let's talk about this tomorrow." She sighed. She walked out of the kitchen and started towards the bedroom. "I'm going to bed. I'm exhausted, and I have an early day tomorrow."

As Dixon watched his fiancé stroll up the stairs with her phone, a wave of disappointment washed over his face while he tore his planner in half, rage overwhelming him so much that his body began to shake.

Every time he tried to speak to her after that, she made an excuse. She had work, she wasn't feeling well, she had a call. Dixon even tried to call Zoe's mother to see what was going on, but the woman seemed just as content to ignore him as her daughter was.

His favorite excuse she came up with was that her chakras weren't aligned so she couldn't make the best decision for them. He'd been so stunned that she hadn't even argued about it. Not that he liked the arguments.

No, this was worse. She flat out ignored him, almost like he was a nobody to her.

The only thing that didn't change was her insistence that they wait a couple of years before officially tying the knot. She acted as if they'd only been together for four weeks. She couldn't even commit to keeping the engagement ring on her finger, the ring he had spent thousands and thousands of dollars on, only wearing it when he asked her to.

After weeks of waiting, he finally had enough. He was tired of walking on eggshells around Zoe and her bullshit, and he was tired of his entire family asking him about their wedding date when he wasn't even sure she still wanted to be with him. He loved his family and didn't want to disappoint them or show any sign that his relationship was struggling before he definitely needed to.

"Zoe," he said one day as she came in the front door. He was leaning against the door frame that led into the living room. "We need to talk."

"I can't. I have to take a shower, and then I'm heading out with some friends from work. I don't have time to talk about this again," she told him as she pushed past him.

Dixon shook his head and grabbed her arm. "No, not this crap again. We're talking. Right here and now. I want to know why you've been distancing from me lately or why you refuse to set a date for the wedding," he told her, trying to keep himself under control. "It doesn't make sense. You said yes, and you were so excited to start planning it and then…it just changed. You stopped caring and started to change your mind about everything, about us. What's wrong with you? We need to talk through this. We're in a relationship. We should be able to talk through things without shutting each other out."

Zoe Bryn rolled her eyes and went into the bathroom. "Nothing's wrong. I don't want to talk. That's it," she told him with a bored sigh.

She turned on the shower and started undressing.

He stood outside the door and shouted in, "I know something's wrong! We've been together for far too long for me to not notice when something's bothering you." He balled his hands into fists. "You can always talk to me. I'm your fiancé."

She sighed and stepped into the shower. She was bent on ignoring him. She had done it plenty of times before.

Dixon dropped his forehead against the door and closed his eyes.

"Zoe, please," he called through the door, knocking on it.

"Go away, Dixon!" she shouted.

He shook his head and pushed away from the door. He leaned against the opposite wall, deciding to wait for her to come out. He knew that he couldn't just let it be.

Something was wrong. He could feel it. And he needed answers.

It took forty minutes before the door opened again, and as soon as she saw him, her shoulders fell.

"Christ, Dixon, I just want to be left alone," she groaned.

She started to head towards the bedroom, gripping the towel around her chest.

"I just want to understand," he nearly begged, reaching for her hand.

"Leave me alone," she said, jerking her hand away.

He stared at her in disappointment, feeling something burning in his chest.

"If you don't give me a reason right now, then I'm calling off the wedding," he told her.

Slowly, she turned towards him, glaring.

"You're going to what?"

"You heard me. I'm calling off the wedding," he said with a simple shrug. He crossed his arms over his chest and looked down at her. "All you have to do is tell me what's wrong, and I won't do it."

"Are you threatening me, Reid?"

"If that's what you want to call this," Dixon responded coyly.

She eyed him for a long minute, and then he saw her shoulders relax. She turned around and walked to the bedroom. He frowned and followed her.

"Well? Aren't you going to talk to me?"

"No." Zoe pulled on a dress. "Feel free to cancel. *If* you want, I'll even foot the bill for the deposits you can't get back." She turned around and began applying her makeup.

Her tone was way too calm. "You never wanted to marry me, did you?" he realized. "Why say yes then?"

Zoe turned around. "You asked me in a restaurant, in front of people. There was too much pressure. I couldn't say no. I would've looked like an asshole. What would you have done?"

"I would have told you I was unhappy."

"Like you ever listen to me."

"You don't tell me anything; how could I listen? You keep hiding things from me, don't talk, don't let me even look at your phone."

Zoe fluffed her hair and tried to leave the room, but he stopped her.

"No, you're not leaving until you answer me. Why don't you want us to get married? We've been together for four years. What changed? Give me a damn reason!"

She balled her hands into fists, and her face started to go red.

"Fine, here's a reason. I'm cheating on you," she told him. She laughed and shrugged. "Happy? That's the big fucking secret. I'm cheating on you, and there's nothing you can do about it. I don't fucking love you anymore. I haven't for years."

Dixon's face fell. Everything around him felt like it was caving in towards him, and he wanted to shove it all away. He stared at her, all the light in his eyes gone.

"You're not cheating me," he whispered.

"I am. I'm going to his place now." She laughed. "Haven't you noticed that I've been going out more?"

"Why?" he asked, his face broken like a sad puppy.

"I'm bored," she groaned. "You're boring, and frankly, pathetic. It's the same thing every week. We do nothing all week, and then on Thursdays, we get to be a couple. I want to do more than just sit around the apartment all week, Dixon. I'm sorry you had to find out this way."

"How long has this been going on?" Dixon was afraid for her answer, but part of him needed to know how long she had been playing him.

"Not that long. Maybe two years?"

"Two years? You've been cheating on me for *two fucking years*? Why the hell did you say yes to the engagement then? Why string me along when you're sleeping with another man?" Every part of his body began to tighten. "I want you out. *Now*. Take your shit, and get the fuck out of my apartment!"

She walked over to him and tapped his cheek with her lips, almost as her way of taunting him.

"Gladly," she said sweetly as she pushed him aside.

Dixon flinched when she touched him and took a step back.

"I can't believe you would do something like this," he whispered. "Honestly. I just...I feel sick to my stomach. You strung me along for two years. Two fucking years."

"You've strung me along for four."

"Don't you want to fix this?" he called.

"Fix *what*?" Zoe finally screamed. "I did everything I was supposed to do. I stood by you when you were broke. I played the good little girlfriend. I made sure you didn't stray when women started paying attention to you after you got famous. I stuffed myself into this box I didn't want to be in, hoping that it's going to be enough. Well, you know what? It isn't! You don't want me; you only want to be with me because of the time you spent on me, so you wouldn't feel like such a loser knowing this relationship was a complete waste of time."

"That's not true."

"Really? Tell me one good reason why we should get married that has nothing to do with how long we've been together."

Dixon opened his mouth. But nothing came out.

"I don't want to be with someone just because of a sunk cost fallacy. I want to be desired, wanted. Don't you think I deserve that?"

Dixon watched her walk out of the bedroom. He knew he should have stopped her. Fought for her. But what was the point?

Maybe she was right. He loved her with everything he had, but he couldn't fight to make her stay if she didn't want to. Any reason she had for leaving was much stronger than any reason he had for her staying.

Besides, she always did whatever she wanted to. Hell, he did whatever she wanted to. Part of the reason why he felt he needed to fix it was because, deep down, he knew he would have never taken his job seriously if she hadn't pushed him. She was the ambitious one. He might have been the one to set the weekly dates, but she controlled everything else.

He'd stopped talking to all of his female friends because of her; he'd stopped working with female producers. But that was okay, because he thought she was scared he'd leave her. He was willing to do anything to make their relationship work.

But she'd been cheating on him for two years.

He didn't even know with who.

Dixon began pacing in their apartment. He should have known something was wrong as soon as she began going out so much. She always said it was a waste of time every time he wanted to go out. He couldn't even recall the last time he'd gone out for a simple beer with his friends. And yet, she had the gall to say *she* was bored?

Dixon stopped pacing. He was in the living room now. Looking at the artfully designed space, the space he thought they had built together because they cared about each other. The vintage armoire she swore reminded her of her great grandmother. The kitchen island she had him build to match the marble countertops. Even the dangling chandelier that cost him an entire leg to buy.

All useless materials that meant nothing now.

Four fucking years. Dixon strode to the bar in the corner, grabbed the scotch, and started drinking. There was enough alcohol in the apartment for him to get blackout drunk several times over.

Maybe this would make sense once he woke up with a hangover.

Somewhere around his seventh glass, the walls began mocking him. He threw the glass at a photo of him and Zoe, arms around each other, laughing. When the frame fell to the floor, he felt better. So, he got up, and stumbled to the rest of them. He threw them all on the ground, stomped on them, then moved on to everything she had ever made him buy.

Soon, the floor was covered in glass shards. He stopped at slicing the couch cushions open. Even in that state, he knew he shouldn't handle anything sharp. He settled for throwing empty bottle after empty bottle at the walls.

* * *

The next morning, he woke up on the ground, more hungover than he had ever been. His throat was raw, his face was red, his eyes stung like someone had poured salt in his eyes. And there was a clear path amid the mess in the living room, from the entrance to the bedroom.

Dixon stumbled inside to find Zoe's things gone. He used to get angry at her for leaving dirty piles of clothes all over the floor, but now, there was nothing he wouldn't give to get that back.

He went back to drinking again. Another day, another empty bottle.

Dixon honestly didn't know what to do with himself after the booze ran out. His mother tried to console him, and his friends tried to drag him out to several clubs to get his mind off of her, but nothing worked. He just couldn't understand what was so wrong with him that he was worth cheating on. He was so full of hope and excitement of finally being able to start a family.

It all seemed impossible now.

A lost cause.

If she made him into what she wanted him to be, then why wasn't she happy still?

But that was the thing. Dixon realized a few days after Zoe had finally, ruthlessly, separated every aspect of their lives, from taking her name off the lease on the apartment, thus forcing him to move out, to blocking him on every social media in existence, probably even some he didn't use, that Zoe had tried making him into someone she could be with. Someone she could love. But it obviously hadn't worked.

Did she even love him to begin with? Or did she just see him as a project she could mold into something?

That was when he stopped drinking so much. The painful thought that came with the idea that he was so unlovable that even years of control could not make someone stand him, couldn't be eased with alcohol. Instead, he locked himself in his apartment and didn't leave.

He did answer when his mom called though, since she was worried that he'd off himself. He wasn't that far off, and at least she cared.

But she had to, didn't she?

* * *

One day, four months after that night, while at home and flipping through the channels, a commercial for Silver Lining came on. He was about to change the channel when he heard the words *true love*. That was not something he needed in his life right now. He was tired of scams, false promises of love that only end up draining his bank account instead.

He scoffed at it, and let the remote fall to his chest.

"I swear," a woman the screen called Marissa Sinclair, a slim woman about Dixon's age, said from the screen, "if you don't turn your life around in thirty days with the Silver Lining lens, then you will be guaranteed a full refund. I created Silver Lining after I was left alone and without a purpose. I knew I needed to find something, something that will give me the love I truly deserve, something that can never hurt me, and I knew, instantly, that this was the *perfect* solution. So, I got it inserted and found the love of my life. And you can too."

The screen changed to a romantic dinner on a beach. The woman, Marissa, sat next to a man who looked like he'd walked out of a male model catalogue. But he must have been a great actor, since the affection between the two seemed too real to be true. They weren't acting as if they were being filmed, and they had to get all of the affection on camera. They pretty much looked like they didn't even know they were being filmed.

They looked so...so...in love, something Dixon always wanted for himself.

"The lens will find you your ideal partner, someone who will never leave or hurt you. It will take into consideration the things you never even thought you needed, and craft the perfect person for you. These Zetas will teach you to love again, will teach you to trust once again. Help you though terrible times, and help you believe the world isn't as horrible as you think it is."

Dixon laughed, shaking his head. He switched the channel and laid his head back on the cushions.

"I can't believe someone would market something like that. It's so ridiculous," he mumbled.

He turned on his side and tucked his head under his arm. He glanced around the small apartment he moved into after Zoe left. He couldn't stand thinking about her anymore. He couldn't stand living in a place he shared with Zoe all these years.

He let his eyes slip shut, and he heard another commercial for Silver Lining come on. He groaned and pulled the blanket off the back of the couch and over his head. He was so tired of hearing about love and having other people throw in his face what he didn't have.

The thought of something like a contact lens helping you find true love and find true happiness in the world didn't settle right in his stomach. It didn't make any sense. Love couldn't be controlled.

You can't mess with someone's feelings like that, can you?

But maybe it would help him get over Zoe. At least, teach him how to live without her. If nothing else, it would at least serve as a good distraction, if only for a little while. A big part of why he hadn't even begun to heal was the fact that Zoe had been his first long-term girlfriend, the only girl who ever managed to stay with him for longer than six months.

Maybe it would help to have a simulation of a relationship for once.

He shook his head. No. Was he really that desperate? What kind of people fell for stuff like that anyway?

"Read the testimonials on our website. With over a million users worldwide, find out why no one has taken us up on our thirty-day return policy as of yet."

Curiosity got the best of him, and he shot straight up. He grabbed his phone and quickly searched the lens. The official website came up for it, and he clicked on it. There were studies shown, pictures of how the lens was made, and how the procedure was done. They all seemed simple enough.

And then there were the testimonials. They weren't in written form. They were videos, a whole archive of them, way more difficult to fake. All with people sharing their thoughts right before the lens and thirty days after. Dixon could tell they really did have it installed, due to the silver circle in their eyes, usually the left. Some turned it on and off in front of the camera to show how it worked.

They were all different—different backgrounds, different states of despair, different reasons for not finding love and taking the leap for the lens. Some had given up on love while others just needed support, others like him.

What really struck Dixon was that, in the end, everyone seemed happy with themselves. They talked about an increased sense of self-worth, a new belief in love.

After an hour of reading over every piece of information the site had, he was interested in at least trying it. Especially if there were no known lasting effects, and he could try it out for thirty days with a full refund if it didn't work. In the end, it seemed that there was nothing to lose.

He set up an appointment with the closest clinic and dropped his phone onto the coffee table.

He was insane. People were going to laugh at him. The famous musician who wrote songs for a living, but was so hopeless and pathetic when it came to love that he had to have a fake partner. He should cancel.

And then do what? Drink again? No, Dixon decided, he was trying this. He didn't have to tell anyone about it. All he was going to do was try it out for thirty days, probably realize it doesn't work, and have it removed.

Nothing more and nothing less, nothing different from a couple one-night hookups.

"I've sunk low," he murmured to himself, sinking back on the couch.

He covered his face, trying to hide the sudden shame he was feeling.

He would at least get out of the apartment.

* * *

His appointment was the very next day. Apparently, they installed these lenses fast. Because of the short time frame, Dixon went through maybe five different excuses he could use to cancel. In the end, he paced in front of the clinic for a few minutes before he cursed himself and strode in.

"Dixon Reid, here for an appointment at 9," he blurted out at the receptionist, a small blond woman in her fifties.

She didn't have the lens. Shouldn't she have the lens since she was working here? To promote their business?

Dixon looked down, caught the ring on her finger, and winced.

"Nervous or excited?" she asked.

"Both?"

"That's normal. You can go into treatment room four. The doctor will be right with you."

The inside of the room was a regular doctor's office, with a dentist chair in the middle of it. Dixon spent most of his time pacing in front of it. He'd never been the type to get worried at a doctor's office; he'd been lucky enough to be healthy, but now, his heart threatened to beat out of his chest.

The doctor, a short, plump elderly man, took one look at him and must have realized his panic, because he went into the standard spiel.

"There is no need to be nervous. This is a simple non-invasive procedure, and the lens can also be easily removed. Everyone gets nervous their first time here. It's completely normal."

"How does it work? Like, do I just turn it on, and boom, a virtual assistant pops up but for relationships?" Dixon asked.

The man smiled. "If that's what you need. Most people meet them the regular way. You know, on the streets or at a bar."

The doctor pulled out a tray of lenses. They all sparkled on the metallic tray as he watched the doctor pick one up with a pair of forceps.

Okay, he was doing this. "I know the site says no one has returned the lens, but how do you know it works?"

"I see their faces when they come in for a checkup at the end of the month. I even installed one in my daughter's eye a few months ago."

The doctor pointed to a photo. Dixon could see a young woman smiling. He could see the lens in her right eye, shining, bright as day.

"Now, I will place the lens in this machine." The doctor pointed to a delicate white machine with a barrel at the end of it. It looked expensive and completely innocuous. "And it will help connect the lens to the nerve in your eye. It won't damage your actual eye in any way, and the connections are easily removed, since they go through the corners of your eye. It finds the two parts of your brain it needs to attach to and then slides out," the doctor gestured at a diagram of an eye on the wall. "I will put you under for the procedure, and afterwards, some report a discomfort in their eye that goes away as the lens settle. You can take an over-the-counter pain reliever if it gets too bad. Any will do."

"Right." Dixon's nod was more for himself than the doctor. "And if it doesn't work, you use the same machine to take it out?"

"Yes, the exact same way."

"Okay, let's do it." Dixon decided he was excited.

This was a thing people did, try new things, and see if they work for them. He could be adventurous. And maybe his Zeta would show him something that was missing about Zoe. Maybe he'd even get over her. That was what sat him down in the chair at the end of the day.

The procedure was fast, and Dixon didn't feel any discomfort afterwards. It felt like he had nothing in his eye, actually, not even like a regular contact lens he'd worn for Halloween to get red eyes once upon a time.

"So, I just click the button to turn it on and off?" He hefted the small box in his hand.

"Exactly."

Dixon walked out of the clinic with his hand gripped onto the small remote as he looked around the street. All he had to do was press the button, and he would get the right person for him. It seemed impossible and a little scary, like something out of a sci-fi movie. He couldn't imagine what he would do if it actually worked.

He started walking back towards his apartment, fiddling with the remote in his pocket. All he had to do was press it. Just a simple click, and his life would change forever. His thumb pressed lightly against the smooth button, but not enough to activate it.

Was he insane? He should go back there and tell them to take it out. They could even keep the money.

Suddenly, someone bumped into him as he began to turn around, and he felt the small click of the button and a small shock against his eyes. He blinked a few times and looked around.

Nothing looked different. Well, the sky was a little bit bluer. But that was it.

Nothing had happened. Nothing changed. Nothing stood out to him. Nothing.

It was a scam. He knew it. He just blew all that money on nothing. How pathetic was he? Like a lens could give him the right partner just like that? Now, he had to walk around with the evidence of his stupidity and gullibility right on his face. And he wondered how he never noticed that Zoe had been cheating on him for the past two years.

If these were the things he pulled when left unsupervised, he was no longer surprised.

He growled and gripped the remote. For a short second, he thought about throwing it straight into the dumpster on the other side of the street. He was ready to storm back into that clinic and yell at them, demand they take it out so he could go on with his normal and sad life, but then almost bumped into a woman.

He jumped back quickly, offering an apologetic smile.

"Whoa, there. I didn't see you," he told her.

He looked down at her, and his heart jumped. He swallowed hard and rubbed the back of his neck as he felt his face flush. The woman before him was the most beautiful woman he had ever seen in his life.

She had a bright smile and dimples to go along with it. She was far smaller than him and petite; Zoe was taller than him, and it sometimes made him feel insecure standing next to her.

This girl had brunette hair in soft waves around her face and large blue eyes. It looked like she was saying something, but all he could hear was the rush of blood in his ears, and his heart trying to claw its way through his chest.

"Are you okay?" he eventually asked, realizing that he hadn't spoken in several minutes.

"I'm fine," she told him, tilting her head to the side to look up at him. She giggled a bit and looked away. "I know this might seem a little weird, but..."

"Do you want coffee?" he asked before she could.

She grinned again and bounced on her heels. "I would love some," she admitted. "Are you free right now?"

Dixon nodded quickly. He then gestured his head down the road. "I know a great coffee place not too far from here. My treat," he said, grinning.

She motioned for him to lead the way.

As they started walking, he couldn't stop thinking about how beautiful she was. He didn't even know her name, but he already felt a strong connection to her. He frowned at the thought. He didn't even know her name.

"I don't think I caught your name," he finally confessed to her, going red again.

"I never gave it to you," she told him. She turned her head to look up at him. "What do you think my name is?" she asked.

Dixon thought for a moment, chewing on his bottom lip. She looked so sweet and innocent. It was almost hard to look at. "You look like you're an April."

She giggled and shook her head. "My name is Jade," she told him. She started to twirl a strand of her hair between her fingers. "You think I really look like an April though?"

He shrugged his shoulders and couldn't stop from laughing.

"Yeah," he said. He motioned to her hair and then to her smile. "You've got hair like the sun, and your smile is just so warm. It reminds me of summer. But not the summer where it's too hot to even go outside."

"Ah, so you decided on April...which is spring," she said, unable to hold back a grin. She put a hand on his arm and squeezed. "You look like...a Dixon."

His eyes went wide, and he stopped walking. She stopped and looked at him, giving him an innocent smile. It didn't work on him though. "You must have heard my name from somewhere."

He couldn't believe for one second that she managed to guess his name right. "You did, didn't you? Were you at the clinic?"

Jade shook her head. "I'm just really good at guessing names," she told him. She clasped her hands in front of her and rocked on her heels again. Her skirt caught against her legs every time she went all the way forward and then all the way back. "What clinic are you talking about?"

"You know, the one that puts in the Silver Lining lens," he told her, pointing in the direction she just came from.

When she looked over her shoulder and then back at him with a confused look, he felt embarrassed again. It felt foolish to admit to someone that that was what he was doing.

"I just got it put in today," he mumbled, looking to the awning on the shop behind her. He was afraid she'd leave and didn't want to see him again. "I'm not really sure if it works though." He glanced back down at her. His heart skipped again. "I don't know what the perfect woman looks like, but I think you're close."

As he spoke, someone bumped straight into Jade without even noticing or acknowledging what had happened. Dixon stepped forward and put a hand on his arm to stop him.

"Excuse me," he said, getting the guy's attention.

The man looked down at his hand, then back at him. "What are you doing?" he asked. "Don't fucking touch me."

"You walked into this nice young woman here, and I think it's best you apologize to her," he told him.

He jerked back and looked down when he felt Jade's hand on his arm. He relaxed when he realized that it was just her. "What? Are you okay?"

"It's alright," she told him quietly. "I promise that I'm fine. Really."

Dixon sighed and let the guy's arm go. "Fine," he murmured. He looked at him. "You're lucky she's telling me it's fine, or I would make you apologize."

The stranger looked at him like he was insane. "Whatever you say," he muttered and started walking away. "Fucking weirdo."

Dixon turned back to her and gave her a smile. "Are you sure you're okay? He didn't hit you too hard, did he?"

Jade smiled and walked over to him, taking his hand gently. "How about we get to know each other over a cup of coffee and see how it goes from there?" she suggested, tugging his hand so he would follow.

Dixon couldn't believe that someone as beautiful as her would still want someone like him. He basically just admitted that he was so bad at dating that he needed a miracle contact lens to help him out. This was too good to be true.

He blinked. But wait, maybe she *was* his perfect match, the one the lens promised to give him. Maybe this wasn't by chance at all; maybe this was destiny.

"Okay, okay," he groaned, but a grin was still on his face.

When she started tugging, he let his weight pull against her a bit, feigning reluctance.

"If you keep doing that, then I'll have to just pick you up and carry you to the café," she warned him.

She looked back at him, and he swore he saw a twinkle in her eye. He knew that she was the one. It couldn't be anyone else.

She was too perfect for him.

Chapter Three

Bethany Rose

Bethany Rose didn't believe that there was anyone out there who was made just for her. It was something she had learned from her mother after she jumped from guy to guy without a care in the world. She didn't hate her mother for showing her the harsh reality of the world so early on in life. In fact, she probably loved her mother more for it.

Relationships were not about the perfect soulmate that would love or cherish you forever. They were closer to buses. You found the one who led you closest to where you wanted to be. And the destination was usually slightly happier and less sexually frustrated, nothing more, nothing less.

It's not like people wanted anything more from her anyway. When it came to starting a life with someone, she was always the one who waited around for someone to love her back, someone to treat her the way she treated them.

Even if not, she was usually okay with the men she met treating her like garbage, and that's why they hadn't stopped since. But it wasn't the way to live. No one deserved to live like this, not even her.

She'd been through it with Liam. She had all of her life planned out, just like he wanted. He wanted to move to England, by the water. He never asked if Bethany hated winter and snow, but then again, she never mentioned it either, too caught up in the fact that someone was actually building a life with her to care if she even liked it.

And it had no bearing on how he decided he then wanted to travel the world, dumped her by moving out in the middle of the night without even a note, and left her stuck in a place she hated.

After seven years of living together.

But she'd managed on her own. She found a job she liked alright. She had friends now, a nice apartment in the middle of the busiest part of the city, and she was happy, as happy as she could be in a situation like this. After all these years, she finally learned to accept the truth about love.

She would never change herself for a partner ever again. She had been burned too many times to walk back into that trap.

It meant that she didn't have to waste her time searching for the person who gave her butterflies or made her smile so much her cheeks hurt. She was fine with using social media and dating apps. It was like an endless supply of men who were willing to have a no strings attached one-night stand.

She spent her whole life chasing after the dream of the perfect husband and family that she lost herself in the process. Now, it was time for her to take her life back and just enjoy life.

She didn't think there was anything wrong with it even if others did. She had enough people in her life telling her that what she was doing was wrong. Giving women a bad name, like her life had any bearing on their own decisions. She kindly gave them all the middle finger and told them to let her do what she pleased with her body. They didn't like that though and only attacked her more.

However, it wasn't something she could let get to her. She was living her life the way she wanted, and she was happy.

Plus, she didn't have time for a relationship even if she wanted one. She managed a hotel for a living. Work took up most of her time with long hours of overtime and, occasionally, unexpected overnight trips out of town to the other locations the hotel had worldwide. It was a little annoying to deal with, but she knew that she couldn't complain. The pay was amazing.

But some people wouldn't let it go. And some meant well.

Thea, her long-time best friend, tossed a magazine in front of her one day. "Look at that," she told Bethany. "I think you might like it."

Bethany raised an eyebrow at her before showing her the picture of a laxative ad. "Are you trying to tell me something?" she asked, trying not to laugh. "I have so many questions. The first being, how do you even know they work?"

Thea rolled her eyes and snatched the magazine back from Bethany. "That's not what I wanted to show you," she mumbled as she flipped the page over. A smile curled up at the edge of her lips when she found it. She showed Bethany again. "This. The Silver Lining lens."

Bethany frowned at her friend as she looked at the photo of a brunette with a dazzling smile and one silver eye, then shook her head. "That thing looks ridiculous," she told Thea. Bethany took the magazine back so she could get a closer look. "Find true love and happiness?

What does that even mean? Come on, Thea, we both know true love doesn't exist."

"It means…you'll find true love and happiness." Thea laughed in return. She moved closer so she could look at the ad. She pointed to the bottom of the page. "It helps you find the one person you're meant to be with. I'm sort of tempted to do it myself."

"You're married, remember?" Bethany reminded her. She then turned and gave Thea a look. "With kids. I don't think you should be running around talking about finding the true love of your life. You've already found him."

Thea rolled her eyes dramatically and tossed the magazine into her lap. "I know, I know, I'm lucky." She sighed, waving the comment off. She tapped the glossy paper. "You haven't though. And I'm sure you're tired of sleazy men like Liam who make you fake promises and then take them all away."

"I don't want to." Bethany sighed. She dropped the magazine on the coffee table as she headed towards the kitchen. "I'm happy with how I am. I don't know how many times I have to tell you that. I thought you would have gotten that through your head by now."

"Oh, I get it," Thea said as she quickly got up to follow Bethany, standing behind her as she started a pot of coffee. "But I think you would still benefit from having even one healthy relationship."

Bethany stopped and turned to face Thea, tapping her chin in thought. "I think I already had one of those. It was the third grade, and I was dating this kid called fuck you," she deadpanned. She laughed as Thea threw a dishtowel at her. "What? It's true. His first name was Fuck, and his last name was You. I can't make things like this up."

"I'm going to strangle you in your sleep," Thea mumbled, shaking her head.

Bethany narrowed her eyes at her friend. "Do you watch me sleep? Because if you do, that would explain why you think I need laxatives."

"Will you please just try it? For my sake, at least?" Thea nearly begged.

"The laxatives?" Bethany asked, raising an eyebrow.

She was thoroughly lost in their conversation now.

Thea groaned and dropped into a seat at the dining room table. "You're impossible," she mumbled as she put her head on her arms, laying against the table.

Bethany walked over to her and kissed her head. "Ah, but you love me," she said quietly. "Maybe you're my one true love."

"Please, I may love you, but you sure as hell don't love me," Thea muttered, not bothering to look up at her. "Can you promise me that you're going to look into it? I'm tired of seeing you throw your life away on these meaningless hookups who just use you for your body."

Bethany sighed and let her shoulders fall. She couldn't believe she was even considering it. But she didn't want to disappoint her friend, so she shrugged and sat down across from her.

"I'll think about it. Do some research of my own besides just looking at the stupid ad."

Thea perked up instantly. "Oh, thank you." She grinned. "I bet you'll find out that it actually works and want to use it."

Bethany rolled her eyes. She was fine. Just fine. Sometimes she had a deep craving for someone to just hold her or a deep urge to just smash everything in her apartment and start over, but that was normal.

No one was satisfied all the time. She had accepted her life for what it was and made peace with it.

She did believe that there was someone out there for most people. She had to in order to believe that Thea's relationship was not doomed to failure before it even began. But she was pretty sure her perfect partner was not real. Years and years of endless searching had taught her that. The best she ever hoped to get was someone who could tolerate her.

She watched her friend, shaking her head slowly. She couldn't believe what she was agreeing to.

"I don't understand why you want me to get it so badly," she told Thea as she leaned forward. She propped her elbows against the table and set her chin on her hands. "Care to give me a good explanation?"

"I already told you why I think you should do it," Thea said quietly. She pushed her hair back off her forehead and gave Bethany a weary smile. Thea glanced at the coffee just as the machine dinged. "I want you to have a healthy, stable relationship, that's all. I've seen you cry after every breakup, chase after every man you fall head over heels for, that I just want you to be happy. I also think it will help give you something else to focus on besides work and whether you'll wake up in your own place the next morning."

Bethany groaned and shook her head. "I do focus on things besides work and sex," she reminded Thea. She motioned around her apartment.

Her apartment was her masterpiece. She had designed and decorated every inch of it all by herself. When she wasn't working or out sleeping with guys, she was working on building her home into an artistic masterpiece. She constantly re-imagined it and changed it to match the ever-changing times.

"Your apartment isn't a living, breathing person though. You can't have a relationship with it," Thea reminded her.

Bethany groaned again, shaking her head. She just wanted the conversation to end already.

"Fine," she said, though she didn't sound too happy. "I'll check it out. I'll do as much research as I can, find out that it doesn't work, and that will be the end of it. I hope you're ready for an 'I told you so' when this all blows up in your face."

"Almost a billion people own one already," Thea told her. Thea crossed her legs as she watched her get her coffee ready. "And that's all over the world. I don't think someone can sell something that doesn't work to a billion people."

"Almost a billion."

Thea rolled her eyes. "I'm just happy you're looking into it," she admitted.

"You're a strange woman who finds happiness in the oddest of places," Bethany murmured. She set her mug in front of her before taking her own seat. "Alright," she said as she pulled out her phone, "what's this thing called again?"

"Oh, right now?" she asked, her eyes getting wide. She jumped up. "Let me get the magazine."

Bethany opened the site, just to get it over with. She rolled her eyes at the reviews. A bunch of lovesick idiots with a bunch of stupid cliches. One month is not enough time to guarantee a solid relationship, much less a future.

"Do you really think I'm this desperate?" She gestured at a video of a sobbing woman.

"No, but you need something other than kicking another one-night stand jerk out of your apartment," Thea quickly responded.

Bethany switched over to the tech specifications. "This sounds like science fiction. What happens if they upgrade stuff?"

"They can easily take the lens out." Thea pointed at the section of the site where a video of the removal could be seen.

Bethany scoffed. "Like they'll show a video of it going wrong. This seems like just another marketing scheme." She scrolled down the site. What caught her eye was the section of Zeta biographies. "Huh, the inventor has one. Blaise, his name is?" Bethany said.

At least the inventor looked... normal. An average-looking woman sick of men. And while the partner looked too much like a model for Bethany's taste, he wasn't there to just look pretty, according to the video where he talked about his job as an engineer.

Thea seemed satisfied with Bethany's investigation and didn't mention anything else about it for a week. But she didn't need to.

Bethany kept checking the site on her own. She even checked other sites to see if she could find something wrong with it. She checked for lawsuits, for misdemeanors, and even found information for every staff member she could. She needed to find something wrong with this to stop thinking about it.

She couldn't. She spent hours digging through all the information she could find, even called a friend that she'd met through her work to try and see if anything would pop up. The search led to a phone call, and suddenly, Bethany found herself in front of a nondescript building in the middle of the busy city, debating on whether she really was going to get a freaking lens installed.

Eventually, she grew tired of pacing in front of the clinic. What would her coworkers think about it? The silver glow wasn't that subtle.

"It's okay, you can easily turn it off," she reminded herself. With that, she walked in.

Sitting in the dentist chair was nerve-racking enough with all the unfamiliar equipment scattered around and the ghost of the inevitable phrase, *You're bleeding because you don't floss.* Bethany couldn't think of anything worse than something like that.

Until just recently, that was. She found out that sitting in one when you weren't at the dentist and, in fact, at a clinic to get a contact surgically implanted in your head was worse, much worse.

She couldn't get the sound of drilling out of her head the entire time she was waiting for the doctor to show up. Thankfully, when the doctor did walk in, she had a nice, soothing smile. It helped ease a bit of her nerves.

"Good morning, Ms. Rose." The doctor smiled. She was in her forties, with a childish smile and a halo of brown curls around her head. "How are you feeling?"

"Like I'm about to get all my teeth pulled out," Bethany admitted, looking over at the doctor. She patted the arm rests on the seat. "Why am I in a chair like this anyway? I thought surgeries were supposed to be done lying down."

The doctor smiled as she started to get everything ready. "This is a bit different than normal surgeries," she explained. She pulled down a large white device that looked as if it had a barrel at the end of it. "This is going to do most of the work for me. All I'm doing is cleaning the area, telling you about the procedure, and operating it. You look nervous. Don't worry, everyone is nervous when they first walk in. It's perfectly natural."

Bethany eyed the machine distastefully. She tried to figure out how it worked, but there was nothing but a smooth shell covering everything inside. "How does this work?" she asked.

"Well, I place it over your dominant eye and then press a button. Tiny little robotic arms will come out, place the Silver Lining in, and then it will work its way through the corners of your eye. It finds the two parts of your brain it needs to attach everything to, and then they smoothly slide out," the doctor explained as best she could, pointing out on herself where everything would be taking place.

"Will it hurt?" Bethany decided to ask. "I also wear contacts on a daily basis. Will the lens pierce through my contacts to get to my eye? What if I need to take my contacts out at night?"

"You will be given a drug to put you under for the procedure, but afterwards, you may feel a slight discomfort in your eye. Not everyone feels it, but either way, we send you home with some low-grade painkillers. The discomfort should go away in a couple days, nothing too debilitating. And don't worry about the contacts. Silver Lining will attach pretty stably to your eye. You simply wear your regular contacts over it and can take them out when you need to. It won't affect the lens at all."

"Low-grade," Bethany complained with a small playful smile.

She was trying to get herself to feel better. It seemed so...fake. How was all of this supposed to happen within an hour without anything but slight eye pain?

"I would love to give you something stronger, but we don't ever need it. We've inserted the lens into thousands of customers, and no one has ever come back complaining of pain." The doctor shrugged. "Do you have any more questions before the procedure starts?"

Bethany bit her lip before shaking her head. "I don't think so," she whispered. She looked up one more time at the machine that would be going into her eye. She swallowed hard. "Actually, I have one question."

"What is it?" the doctor asked as she walked over to her with the cleaning supplies and needle.

Bethany pointed up at the machine. "Has this, or any model of this, ever gone haywire inside someone's head, and...I don't know...turned their brain to mush?"

"Only one time," the doctor joked, "but that guy is still alive. Vegetative, but still alive." She smiled.

Bethany glared at her. "Not funny."

"I know, I know." The doctor sighed. She smiled down at Bethany and held up the needle. "I'm going to inject you with this, and then you'll be out like a light in no time. Do you want any music on?"

"Will it matter?" Bethany asked, eyeing the needle.

The tip of it caught the light, and it looked even more menacing, taunting her under the light.

"You won't hear a single thing while you're out, but it might be nice to go to sleep to some soothing sounds and wake up to it, almost like you just had a peaceful and calming dream," the doctor explained. She stuck the needle into Bethany's arm before pushing the plunger down. As soon as the liquid in the needle retracted itself, the doctor tossed it into the sharps bin. "So...music, or no?"

Bethany smiled and closed her eyes. "I'll take some music," she shrugged. Her head was already feeling heavy, like she couldn't move it.

The doctor smiled and held up two CDs. "Heavy metal or pop?"

Bethany opened her mouth, but her words came out jumbled as the drug took a hold of her and pulled her into its dark, empty clutches.

People were jumping all around her. It looked like one of the parties she used to go to when she was young enough to have fun without worrying about getting up in the morning with consequences.

Another blink, and she realized she was at a concert.

Hands wound around her waist, and she was pulled into a very warm hug. She turned around and got lost in warm brown eyes. She couldn't see the man clearly, but she knew he took her breath away. They moved along to the music, the man singing in her ear.

She fell backwards in a lounge chair, at the beach, next to one of the hotels she managed, the sun caressing her skin. She felt calm and relaxed as hands helped her with the sunscreen on her back.

She was a bride now, standing in front of an archway filled with white roses in a beautiful golden gown, sharing vows with the same man, who looked at her with his heart in his eyes.

A cymbal crash made her jolt a bit. When Bethany woke up again minutes later, heavy metal sounded like it was playing off in the distance. Oh, that explained the hazy nature of her dream. She tried to look around, but everything was still blurry from the drugs. Her head pounded as she tried to sit up, and a low groan escaped her.

The music stopped, and the doctor from earlier walked over to Bethany, putting her hand on Bethany's shoulder.

"Stay down, please" the doctor told her.

It sounded like she was underwater. Bethany tried to reach up to her, but her hands didn't feel like her own.

"What happened?" she asked, trying to focus her eyes on the doctor.

"You're just coming out of your procedure," the doctor explained, pushing Bethany's hair back. She shined a light in both of Bethany's eyes before clicking it off. "How are you feeling?"

Bethany shook her head. "Pain," she told her, moving her hand to rub her head. "I need the good stuff, Doc. Really badly."

The doctor shook her head and laughed quietly. "Let me get that for you," she said as she went over to the cabinet. She came back with a small bottle of aspirins. "You can take eight of these home."

Bethany groaned and let her head drop back against her chair. "Just eight of them?" she asked, blinking at the bottle.

She sighed and closed her eyes, taking in a few deep breaths to center herself again.

The doctor laughed quietly and nodded. She dropped eight of them in a prescription bottle and put them in a small bag for Bethany to take home with her. She then sat in her seat and watched as Bethany slowly became aware of her surroundings again.

"Trust me, you won't need any more than that," the doctor finally said. "Are you ready to go over the final step?"

"What else is there to know?" Bethany asked, slowly sitting up.

It didn't hurt as much as she thought it would, and she wasn't as dizzy as before. She turned and looked as the doctor held out a small remote.

"There is one button. It turns on the Silver Lining, and it turns it off, same button for both," she explained. "But in order for it to work, you always have to have it with you. It's sort of like...the power source for the Zetas."

"I thought I was the power source," Bethany mumbled, taking the small remote. She studied it closely, but there really was only one button, nothing else to really look at. "Does it need batteries?"

The doctor shook her head. "Nope," she grinned. She tapped the side of it. "You are the power source for the lens, of course, but this...I guess, is like a cell phone tower. I don't know how else to explain it. I'm sorry. I'm just the messenger."

"I think I get it," Bethany said slowly. She let out a small laugh and tossed it in the air "That's pretty cool. When do I have to press it?"

"Whenever you want." The doctor smiled. "And you never have to shut the lens off. You'll be able to live as normally as you have before. Everything will just become better. You'll see that you can eat better, sleep better; you'll feel better."

"What if I want to shut it off? That's still an option, right?" Bethany asked.

"Then all you have to do is press the button again," the doctor explained. She crossed her one leg over the other as she watched Bethany examine the remote more closely. "Any other questions?"

Bethany nodded quickly and pointed to her eye with the lens in it. "Do I really have thirty days to return this if I don't like it or if it doesn't work?"

"Thirty days with a full refund," the doctor told her. She held up a finger before the patient could say anything else. "But I don't think you'll need it. I have performed thousands of these procedures, and not a single client ever came back. I think you'll find out how much you love it as soon as you walk out of here."

Bethany nodded slowly and examined the remote again.

"I'll hold you to your word," she told the doctor. She stood up from the chair and took the bag of pills from the doctor's hand. "Thank you."

"No, thank YOU," the doctor said with a warm smile. She walked Bethany to the door and clasped her hands behind her back. "I hope that when I see you again, you'll be even happier and not in here."

Bethany laughed quietly. "That's the hope," she said.

She gave a small wave before walking out of the clinic.

On her way home, Bethany decided that she couldn't wait any longer. She wanted to see how much everything would change after pressing the button. She was a little skeptical, but she had read enough scientific journals on how it worked and reviews from people who had already received it. She was ready to see it all for herself.

She closed her eyes and pressed the button. There was a small jolt on the side of her head that made her jump, but nothing else felt different. After taking in a few breaths to steady herself, she opened her eyes.

The world around her seemed to pop in a way that it didn't before, more vibrant and livelier. The air smelled cleaner. The birds were chirping a little louder. It all seemed so real.

Not that it wasn't real before. This was a different kind of real.

She started walking again, looking at everything that surrounded her. She was so distracted by everything that she almost didn't realize she was almost home.

The entire city was a totally different city. It had to be. Her city was never this clean.

A thought suddenly popped into her head and stopped her right in her tracks. What if she was still sedated in the doctor's chair, and everything around her was actually just a dream? It would make sense. More sense than the actual lens changing her world.

Shit, what if she was still *in* the chair? Or what if the lens just mind controlled her instead of making any difference in her life? In anyone's life?

Bethany clicked the button to turn off. A jolt later, the world clicked back to what she knew was reality. She toyed with the clicker for a while, then stopped.

What if she broke it? She didn't want to get stuck with only one option. Bethany turned to look at herself in a store front, the silver ring barely but still noticeable. This was ridiculous; she looked ridiculous.

Bethany clicked the lens to on and tipped her head back to dip a finger into her eye. She wore contacts all the time, so she knew how to take them out of auto pilot, but the lens didn't budge.

Shit, what if the lens was stuck in her eye?

Bethany felt herself panicking and tried to take deep breaths. It was supposed to be stuck in her eye, she had read. It had wires. That's how the lens work.

Bethany turned her head around from her reflection, and the world turned back into a small circle, the perfect world she had just seen minutes before. Her eyes shot towards a corner when she saw a man turning and walking in her direction.

He was tall and wide, well-built, but not like he spent all his time at the gym. But what really took her by surprise was the calmness on his face, the warm brown of his eyes, and the soft smile on his face. Her mouth hung open so much that she was sure she would have to pick it up off the ground. He didn't seem to notice or care because he was walking right to her.

Not in her direction.

To her.

"Hey beautiful," he said softly, his large eyes shining in the early afternoon sun.

Bethany didn't know what came over her when she giggled, but she did, and she quickly covered her mouth right after. She wasn't the giggling type. That just wasn't how she was. She swallowed hard before lowering her hand.

"Hi."

"I'm Haven," he told her. He glanced around as he stuck his hands in his jean pockets. "I saw you, and...well, I don't usually do this...I just thought you were so beautiful. I couldn't help but admire you. I decided to be bold for once and step outside my comfort zone so... here I am."

She bit her lip, staring up at him. He was unbelievably cute. He blinked at her expectantly, and she blinked back.

When she realized that he was waiting for her to say something, she quickly straightened herself up and gave him a shy smile. She didn't understand what had just come over her.

"I'm Bethany," she finally told him. "Bethany Rose."

"Well, Bethany Rose," he said, holding out a business card. "I would like to take you out sometime. I know it seems a bit forward, but like I said, I'm stepping outside my comfort zone."

Her stomach flipped at the sight of it. A business card usually meant that he either ran his own business or was very high up the corporate ladder at another.

"It's not forward at all," she assured him. She took the business card and read over the details. "I'm used to...never mind about that."

He laughed softly and watched her as she looked at the card again. "You can text me whenever you're free," he told her. "Or call, if you prefer. I've got to go now though; otherwise, I would stay and talk your ear off."

"Oh, that's fine," she said quietly. She motioned down the street a bit. "I don't live far from here, and that's where I was heading. I'll call you though. Definitely."

"Perfect," he hummed. He gently touched her arm and smiled softly before walking around her. He turned and started walking backwards. "I'll be patiently waiting for your call, Bethany Rose."

"I won't make you wait too long," she promised.

Haven turned back around and started walking away. Bethany tilted her head as she struggled to take her eyes off him, admiring every little detail she could from just his backside.

When he was out of sight, she smirked and flicked the business card with her finger. She wouldn't mind trying to date another executive. It probably meant both of their schedules were just as busy, and neither one would get upset over the other for not being home.

If it didn't work out, then oh well. She was sure the lens would be able to find her another man. Or she would just return it. She was excited for it to work though.

As soon as she told Thea, she knew she would be getting an earful of, "I told you so." She could just not tell her about it. It would make things easier and allow her to navigate her new relationship herself.

Though, it wasn't a relationship yet.

Only a date.

Chapter Four

Date with Destiny

The coffee date lasted the entire day. Dixon never had so many muffins at once. He felt like his stomach was about to explode after shoving that last chocolate chip muffin into his mouth, but he didn't care. He was too distracted by the woman sitting in front of him, glowing bright like the sun itself.

Jade was a kindergarten teacher in between jobs. She had never heard about his music, so he didn't need to worry about her being a fan. She loved plants, and she always wanted a big family, just like him.

He couldn't look away from her; she was calm, didn't gesture a lot with her hands like Zoe always did, and had a soft smile that didn't seem to leave her face. And she made corny jokes that made him laugh for days at a time.

The second date was the very next day. They went to see a movie he'd wanted to see for a while, but he spent more time looking at Jade than anything else.

He explained the plot to her afterwards at a small restaurant that just opened near him. She spent most of the time with her chin in her hand, observing every aspect of him, her attention only on him. They spent the entire night together, ending it with a walk in the park and ice cream.

His original thought proved to be right. Even if Dixon was madly in love with her just after two dates, he still thought she was too perfect to be real. He wouldn't dare tell her just in case she decided to get up and leave. He knew that if she left, he wouldn't be able to go on anymore. It wouldn't be like when Zoe left him either; he knew, deep down, that he would be devastated, no longer finding a reason to continue his life.

When he had the lens inserted, the doctor assured him that his Zeta would forever be loyal. But could he really trust him? What if he was wrong, and Dixon lost Jade before he could even say, "I love you?"

They had only gone out two times, but he felt like he'd known her all his life. It just recently dawned on him that the Silver Lining lens had worked. It found his one true love. The one person he could finally be happy with.

It not only worked in finding her, but everything else around him felt lighter also. Work wasn't stressful anymore, and his family became much less aggravating; nothing bad happened to him anymore, and everything seemed to be falling into place.

Dixon couldn't stop thinking about how wonderful his life was while he waited for Jade to show up for dinner one night. This was finally the night where he would bring her back to his place.

He sat alone at the restaurant bar and was about to order another water. He didn't want to start drinking until she got there, when he felt a tap on his shoulder.

"Well, it's about time," he teased as he turned around in his chair.

His smile dropped instantly when he didn't see anyone there. His brows furrowed together as he shook his head.

Maybe someone had just bumped into him on their way to a table. He swiveled back around and leaned his elbows against the bar.

"Can I get another water?" he asked the bartender.

There was another tap on his shoulder. He swung around again. There was definitely someone touching him. His eyes darted to the door when he saw Jade walk in. She waved at him, and he hurried to get up and greet her. The waiter pointed out their table to them, and they walked over.

Jade didn't like him pulling out her chair for her. It made her clumsy, she'd said, so he just sat down.

Dixon grinned as Jade slipped into the chair right next to him. He took her hand and kissed it gently.

"Hello," he hummed. He propped his foot up on the bridge of her chair and rested their hands on his knee. "God, you look gorgeous tonight."

Jade blushed and looked away. "That's what you said the last two times we've seen each other," she reminded him.

He laughed as he dropped his head forward. "I know, I know." He sighed. He squeezed her hand again. "I just can't help it, honestly. Every time I see you, I'm..." he had to find the right word for how he felt, but he didn't think he would ever be able to. Instead, he settled with, "...amazed by how beautiful you are."

She leaned over and kissed his cheek. "You're so sweet," she whispered, gently cupping his cheek. "I'm so lucky that I met you."

"I was thinking the same thing," he admitted, squeezing her hand again.

He admired her with gentle eyes, never wanting to stop. He knew that if he could spend every moment of his life just watching her smile, he would die a happy man.

His thought was interrupted when their waiter arrived in front of him, holding two glasses.

"Your waters, sir," he said politely.

"Should we order something to eat?" Jade asked, turning back to the table as their drinks slid in front of them.

"Yes," he practically moaned. "I've been starving since lunch. The tuna salad I had was amazing, but I knew I was coming out with you, so I wanted to save some room for dinner."

She reached over and patted his stomach. She looked up at him, shaking her head in disbelief.

"You have to eat." She laughed.

"Oh, don't worry about me and food. I never let myself go too hungry." He chuckled. He looked around the room for their server and held up his hand when he saw one. "I've been eating like a king ever since I got the lens. It's like...I know everything that I need to be eating now. It's amazing."

Jade grinned and nodded along. She leaned back as the server came and held back a laugh when Dixon took her hand. She gave it a small encouraging squeeze.

As soon as the appetizer was ordered, Dixon turned back towards the table and their drinks. He glanced at her appletini and noticed that it was already almost empty. He quickly took a few sips just so he could catch up with her.

"I'll have the Antipasto Salad and the Fettuccine Alfredo," he told the server and then turned to Jade. "What do you want?"

"The same, I think," she said.

"Two of those, please." He poked the server, who seemed confused.

"Two, sir? Are you expecting someone?"

"She's already here." Dixon frowned.

Servers at restaurants everywhere had turned a bit weird these days. Was he blind or something?

"Right... Alright, sir, two it is." The server left, shaking his head.

They spent the rest of the night talking and getting to know each other more and more. Dixon wanted to know as much about her as he could, as fast as he could. To him, it felt like they should have been together for years instead of just days, and he was determined to make up for it.

Shortly after they started dating, Dixon proclaimed himself the happiest man alive. Everything had happened so fast that it put him in a sort of daze. He felt like he was stuck in the middle of a movie montage where everything jumped from one milestone to the next.

Jade and him finally made love that night, and they shared their first, "I love you." Not long after, she moved in with him into a new house. Not only were good things happening with Jade, but with work as well.

He got promoted and was praised by his boss for his hard work and dedication. With the extra money and the bonus from his promotion, he was soon able to buy a new house for them.

Everything was falling into place, just the way Dixon always dreamt of. The one thing he had to thank was Silver Lining. Before it, he was miserable and down on his luck in every aspect of his life, leaving him depressed.

Nothing was perfect like it was now. He didn't even know what he was doing different. He just felt happier, healthier. He was more in love and definitely felt more loved than before.

"We should join my parents when they go on their trip to Europe this year," Dixon told Jade one night while they were cooking dinner together. He was chopping the carrots while she checked on the chicken braising in the oven. "It would be nice, and I want them to get to know you. My mom already loves you from what I've told her and can't wait to meet you."

"I think that's only true because *you're* telling her all about me," she told him as she turned to face him. She leaned against the counter next to him and looked up. "But I would be happy to meet them and join them, if that's what you wish."

"Of course, it's what I wish," he said, mocking her word choice. He leaned down and pecked her lips to show her that he was joking before he stood up straight and headed back to the chopping board. "I love you, and I know they'll love you all the same."

She dropped her head against his arm and closed her eyes. "I hope you're right," she said quietly. She started to chew on her bottom lip, letting out a soft sigh.

He frowned and nudged her back gently. "Hey, are you okay?" he asked, tilting her chin up so he could look into her eyes. He could see nothing but worry sitting behind her eyes. "Is there something on your mind?"

"I'm just worried that they won't like me," she simply said. She offered him a small smile before stepping back. "You paint me out to be this perfect woman, but to them, I'll just be some girl their son is in love with. Some girl who is trying to steal him away from them."

A laugh escaped him, and he let his hand drop from her chin.

"Trust me, my parents want you to steal me away. My mom was worried that after my last relationship, I would take forever to bounce back. Actually, when I told her about meeting you, she was so surprised, she almost fainted."

"Oh, that's not good." Jade gasped. He started laughing, and she hit his arm lightly. "How dare you laugh at your mother like that? You should be ashamed. As the future mother of your kids, I order you to call your mother and apologize."

He raised an eyebrow at her. "Future mother of my kids?" he asked, his voice dropping low. He snagged her by the waist and pulled her against him, swaying both of them from side to side. "Since when did that become a thing?"

She blushed and hid her face against his chest. "Not for a little while longer," she told him, hitting his chest lightly. She pulled back and looked up at him. "Just…one day in the future, I want to have kids with you. I want…to have everything with you. You're my future, Dixon Reid."

He smiled down at her and tightened his hold as he leaned down to kiss her. He tilted his head to the side and hummed slightly when she slid her arms around his neck.

When he eventually pulled away, he was grinning and breathing heavily.

"You sure you want to wait?" he asked teasingly.

"Yes, I want you to find where you want to be before we start having a family," she told him.

"And what about you?" he asked, swaying their hips again. "Did you find where *you* want to be?"

She grinned and leaned up on her toes to kiss him again. The kiss caused warmth to spread through his chest, and he wished it would never end.

"I think I have," she whispered as she fell back on her heels.

He grinned down at her, moving them to music that wasn't there. His painful past was barely even a memory for him anymore. With Jade by his side, he knew he would be happy forever.

Chapter Five

Zoe Bryn

Zoe Bryn spotted her ex-fiancé, Dixon, as soon as she walked into the restaurant. He was at the bar, sipping a water of all things, something she never thought she'd witness at a bar. She continued to stare at him; it seemed like his demeanor had changed drastically. There was a wide smile on his face; she could see it from the side, an expression she hadn't seen on his face in years.

Other than that, he seemed the same as before, rumpled shirt, basic pants she probably bullied him into buying, and scuffed shoes. He'd been such low maintenance.

She walked up to him. "Hello, Dixon."

He didn't seem to hear her. She tapped his shoulder. He turned around, and his blinding smile fell into a frown as he looked right through her. She always demanded for his attention, so the lack of it made her freeze, confused. Then he just turned back to his water. Zoe frowned when he ignored her. She put silver hands on her hips.

"Dixon," she called again, this time a little louder.

She tapped his shoulder once more.

He swung around again, retort on his lips. The blinding smile was back, but his eyes were on the entrance. He got up; Zoe had to move so he didn't push her away. She noticed that there was a weird silver ring around his right eye.

When he came back towards her, Zoe watched and followed as Dixon was led over to an empty table, his head constantly turning to the plant next to him.

"Hello." She heard him hum. He propped his foot up on the chair next to him and rested his hand on his knee. "God, you look gorgeous tonight."

Zoe grinned when it finally seemed like he saw her. His eyes lit up, and his smile nearly split his face. Though, when he turned back to the waiter and ordered two martinis, her own smile vanished.

"I don't like martinis, you…"

A woman sat down a seat away from him and smiled at the waiter who walked past her.

"An appletini, please," she told him when she grabbed his attention.

She turned to look at Dixon and gave a small wave.

Zoe let her shoulders drop as she realized that he was probably on a date. She didn't understand why it upset her so much. She was the one to leave him, after all, and she and Scott had been doing really well.

"I can see that you're just going to continue to ignore me. That's fine. I'm not upset or anything," she told him. "Didn't really want to talk to you anyway."

She turned sharply and started back towards the bar. Not without stopping and sizing the other woman up first, though. She was decent, she admitted reluctantly. Slim, long brown hair, piercing blue eyes.

She had a good view of the two of them, lurking from afar without being too obvious, until another couple sat down at a table in front of her, blocking her view. Zoe would have to move if she wanted to spy on Dixon and see what he was up to. She moved chairs, glared at a man who came to chat her up until he left with his tail in between his legs, and observed.

The whole time they sat there, Zoe watched them from the bar, her hands gripping onto her pint glass tightly. She stared at Dixon as he leaned over his drink and his food talking to the woman one seat down from him. It didn't even look like she was paying attention.

What was wrong with this woman? On a date with someone and not even sit next to him?

She knew the only thing Dixon cared to talk about was music, but he was engaging when he did it. Zoe had learned everything she knew about music from him. She wanted to go over and tell the woman to pay attention to him, that she was being rude for texting while on a date.

Then she reminded herself that he'd completely ignored her. It still got under her skin, watching him talking to someone else. It was his fault she left. He was the boring one. The woman he was with clearly knew that as well.

Then, why did she miss him? She couldn't figure it out. Scott was fun and all, strikingly handsome; he took her places, he gave her presents, and he was adventurous in bed. She didn't even need to baby him into getting his life together or nag him constantly. He was everything Dixon wasn't.

But then again, Scott never ignored other women for her. She always needed to keep his attention on her. And he, well, he only ever complimented her on her looks. He never asked her about her work, how her day was, or how she was feeling, something Dixon did way too often, so much that she found him annoying at times.

With Scott, Zoe found herself treating other women like threats a lot more. She was counting down the days until he did something she couldn't forgive, and they'd inevitably fall apart. She never had to do any of that with Dixon.

As she watched him talk to the woman, well, at the woman anyway, she realized why she missed him. He was the only one who ever treated her with any respect. Who had tried to be worthy of her. Why did she just shut him out, so quickly too?

Maybe she could've asked him to be more spontaneous. He always took her desires into account. She shouldn't have cheated on him.

Zoe drained her glass and asked for another beer.

But when the woman next to Dixon got up and walked away, he didn't stop talking. Zoe frowned and looked around, trying to figure out who he could be talking to. There was no one. Everyone else was either on their phone or with another person.

Zoe shook her head as she took a sip of her beer.

Poor bastard had gone insane.

She watched him for another hour, paid her tab, and left. She had already burned that bridge, but she could at least try and fix her life. The first thing was to break up with Scott. Maybe focus on her career for a while. Maybe she could finally find the perfect man for her.

As she walked, a billboard caught her eye.

"Everyone deserves their own loyal Zeta," she read. The billboard had a photo of a couple embracing each other, one of whom had a silver ring around her eye. "Find the love of your life, with Silver Lining," she continued.

That sounded interesting.

She took out her phone and searched through the site. It sounded too good to be true. Which probably meant it was. She thought back to Dixon's silver eye. He probably had one of those. He'd probably been talking to his Zeta. It all made sense now.

However, though it seemed like a great idea, she didn't want to be seen talking to empty air.

She'd rather be with an actual person. That, or she'd rather be alone. It would be nice to know what the perfect partner would be like for her though, but this wasn't the answer to what she was looking for. It would be an illusion.

She didn't want an illusion. Life was a lot more interesting that way.

She quickly disregarded the idea from her head, turned off her phone, and headed home. She'd break up with Scott tomorrow.

Chapter Six

Blinded by Love

The city park was beautiful at night. There was barely anyone there, and the stars shined a little brighter than usual. It wrapped around Bethany and Haven as they strolled beneath the night sky, arm in arm with each other.

Bethany closed her eyes as she leaned against Haven, feeling safe pressed against his side. It was their first date, and she already felt like she was head over heels in love with him. She couldn't be sure though, seeing as she never felt love before. She had only seen it described in books or in movies.

Thea tried explaining it once to her, but she couldn't find the right words that could accurately convey the feelings she felt for her husband. All she said was that there was an overwhelming feeling in her chest any time she saw him.

Well, Bethany thought, if that was love, then she was definitely feeling it. She couldn't believe how easy it was for her to fall for him. She thought it would have been harder. That she would have needed time to trust him. She thought there would have been a longer amount of time before seeing him and loving him. She wanted to tell

Haven how she felt about him, but she didn't want to scare him away. She didn't even know if he would understand why she knew he was the one for her.

"You know," he said after several moments of walking. He squeezed Bethany around her shoulders gently as he looked down at her. "I think I may already be in love with you."

She stopped dead in her tracks, jerking him to a stop as well since he was holding her.

"Really?" she asked, her eyes wide and full of hope. "You think you're in love? With me?"

He nodded, licking his lips. "Is that a bad thing?" he asked, his cheeks blushing red.

A grin split her face, and she jumped up so she could wrap her arms around his neck. "No, it's the opposite of a bad thing," she promised, burying her face in his shoulder. "God. I was just thinking the same thing, honestly. I can't believe how easy it was. I thought that it would take months for us to get to that point, and that was only if we did get to that point."

He slid his arms around her waist and pulled her up into another kiss just to stop her from rambling. They parted seconds later when he loosened his grip, and she fell back, dazed.

"I love you, Bethany."

"I love you too," she whispered back.

* * *

Things only got better as the months passed. They started seeing each other as much as they could around work. Eventually, they started to spend more time with each other than they did anywhere else and with anyone else. Somehow, it worked out so well for Bethany. She didn't have to fight with him, and he was always interested in hearing about her day, even though that information paled in significance every time she saw him.

When things got really serious a month later, she asked him if he wanted to move in with her. Actually, she blurted it out without even thinking about it. The question surprised both of them, but he didn't waste too much time before agreeing.

So, the next day, Haven packed up his things and moved into her place. It would be much easier for him to move his stuff because he barely had anything in his apartment. He was usually out of town a lot since he worked as a consultant, so it didn't matter what was in his apartment.

However, Bethany couldn't stop thinking that it was all too good to be true. It seemed so surreal, like she was living in a fairytale, but real. She was extremely happy, but there was something that kept lurking in the back of her mind that told her she didn't deserve it, and that the love of her life was going to leave at any moment.

She kept pushing those thoughts away though. She didn't want to think about any of them. Haven was there for her any time she needed him. Night and day, no matter where he was. And now, he was home with her.

He was home. She actually had a man living with her. She never expected that to happen again because she never thought she'd let it happen again. Her mother warned her after her last relationship that she should never welcome another man into her home if he was going to stay there.

She was starting to think that her mother was just a cynical woman.

As Bethany was putting away the last of the boxes, she heard a knock on the door.

"I've got it," she called to Haven, who was just in the next room. When she opened the door, she was surprised to see Thea standing on the other side. "Oh, hello. God. It's been ages since I've seen you."

"You're telling me." Her friend smiled at her. "I decided that since you weren't answering my calls or showing up to any of my social events, that I would come around and see if you were okay."

Bethany suddenly realized she hadn't introduced Thea to Haven at all. She used it as a safety mechanism at first, a way to remove pressure from her relationship, but now, it was a little embarrassing.

"I'm fine. Actually, there is someone I'd like you to meet."

"Wait, did you get the procedure done?" Thea asked, entering the apartment.

Bethany nodded and led her into the kitchen.

"Yeah. About a month ago, actually," Bethany admitted. She looked down at her bare feet and shrugged. "I met a guy the same day, and we've sort of been going out a lot. I guess I got distracted. I'm sorry."

She was waiting for Thea's I-told-you-so's.

"Wait," Thea said, holding up a hand. "You met a guy?"

"Yeah, his name is Haven," she told her. She motioned to the dining table. "Have a seat. He's just in the living room."

She walked into the living room to tell him about their visitor.

"Honey, my friend is here. I can't wait for you to meet her."

Haven was on the couch, face buried in a book. He looked up and gave her a tired smile. "I'm sorry, Bethany. Can I take a raincheck? I don't feel up to it right now."

"Oh, well, that's okay, I guess. You can meet her some other time." Bethany frowned a bit.

Why wouldn't he want to meet her friend? Thea was the reason they had met, after all. Bethany shrugged and went back to the kitchen.

"He says he's feeling a little tired," she told Thea. "I'll let him rest. I kept him up most of last night. Maybe another time." Bethany tried for a smirk.

"Bethany, no one was in there," Thea told her.

"What?" Bethany asked and turned back. He wasn't on the couch anymore. "Oh...he's...in the bedroom. He must have gotten up and went upstairs to give us some privacy."

"You just said he was in the living room, and you stood at the couch talking to yourself," Thea whispered. "Are you okay?"

Bethany looked back into the living room. "He *was* on the couch, but he moved when he heard you at the door. He must not be feeling well," she explained. "Also, I was talking to him from down the hall. I'm sorry that you couldn't meet him."

"You've really let this place go, didn't you?" Thea changed the subject.

Bethany's shoulders dropped, and she gave Thea a look. "I did not let this place go. We just finished moving everything of his in, and I'm still trying to get it organized. Did you come here just to question and criticize me?"

Yeah, Bethany could admit that there were a few bags all over the place, and cleaning up didn't seem all that important when she could spend time with someone who made her feel special.

Thea shook her head. "No, no. I didn't. I wanted to make sure everything was okay. I was just a little worried about you. You've been missing for the past month."

Bethany shrugged her shoulder. "I found someone who makes me happy and is taking up most of my time. I've been working less, going out more; I'm having a great time. I thought you'd be happy for me."

"I am happy for you." Thea didn't sound happy.

"It's just his things; it's not like it's garbage."

"I...you're right. You're right. Not garbage. But maybe I can help you clean up some? Help organize. You know how much fun we always have when we do it together."

Bethany shook her head. "No, I think I've got it," she promised. Maybe Haven would like to spend time with them then. Or no, Bethany didn't want Thea to say anything that would make him leave. "I should really get back to fixing up the place. I don't want to lose the energy to do it. How about we set up a date to hang out next week, and you and I will have a girl's night out."

"You better call me, or the next time I show up, I won't be knocking, and I'll make sure you two are in the middle of sex." Thea got up.

Bethany rolled her eyes as she walked her to the door. "If that's what you want to see, then that's what you want to see." She chuckled. "Don't expect me to apologize." She shut the door behind her.

As soon as Thea left, Bethany felt someone behind her. She jumped when Haven touched her shoulder.

"Oh, you scared me." She laughed, putting a hand to her chest. "Why didn't you want to see my friend?" she asked.

"I just wasn't feeling up to it," he told her. "Maybe next time."

"Yeah, maybe next time," she said. She wrapped her arms around his neck and pulled him down for a kiss. She pulled away with her eyes shut. Every kiss with him felt better than the last. "I'm going to start putting your things away," she whispered. "You go lie back down. I promise not to be much longer."

"You better not be," he said in a mock-serious tone.

He then winked at her and walked into the living room.

Bethany couldn't stop smiling. She turned back towards the kitchen and put her hands on her hips as she looked at everything strewn around the room. She rolled up her sleeves before getting to work. There wasn't *that* much of a mess; she'd be done in a few minutes.

She rinsed out a bowl and placed it on the counter. A clink sounded right before the bowl crashed on the floor. Bethany cursed and bent over to clean it up. That was a bit too much porcelain for it to just be a bowl though. She must have knocked over a few plates too. How, she had no idea, but oh well.

"You okay?" Haven came over to help. He grabbed her hand when she cut herself on a shard. "I think that's enough cleaning. Wanna watch a movie?"

"Oh, yes. I can always finish this later."

She let him pull her to her feet. Bethany settled against Haven's chest as she dug the remote out from between the couch cushions and picked a movie out of a list. Something they didn't have to pay much attention to if they got distracted.

Chapter Seven

Thea rang the doorbell and shuffled her feet. She hoped that Bethany wasn't mad at her or anything. The last time they saw each other was when they talked about the lens; maybe Bethany didn't appreciate the meddling and was still mad at her for pushing her into it.

Thea was ready to apologize and take her out to dinner and drinks, if that's what it took.

But when Bethany opened the door, Thea stopped short. She couldn't help but notice how different Bethany looked. Her skin was pale, she was a lot thinner, and there was an odd restlessness about her, like Thea had interrupted something important.

But at least she didn't sound mad.

"I decided that since you weren't answering my calls or showing up to any of my social events, that I would come around and see if you were okay."

"I'm fine. Actually, there is someone I'd like you to meet."

Thea raised an eyebrow at her friend and looked her up and down again. She noticed that one of her eyes had a silver tint to it. That's when Thea figured it out. Bethany had found her perfect guy. She couldn't wait to sit in the kitchen and hear her friend gush about him.

"Wait, did you get the procedure done?" she asked with a laugh.

Bethany nodded and led her into the kitchen. As they walked, Thea took in the surroundings with wide eyes. Bethany had always been meticulous with her space. That wasn't the case right now.

There was garbage everywhere. The smell coming from the food laying out on half-eaten plates on top of almost every surface was really out of place. Bethany had done some dishes, but the kitchen table seemed to have a fine layer of grime on top of it.

"I guess I got distracted. I'm sorry."

Bethany's words got Thea to look at her friend again.

"Wait," Thea said, holding up a hand. "You met a guy?" Had she brought him home yet? Thea hoped not.

Maybe she could help her clean up the mess before the guy saw her apartment for the first time.

"Yeah, his name is Haven," Bethany told her. She motioned to the table. "Have a seat. He's just in the living room."

Thea frowned and glanced into the living room. It was a mess in there too, forgotten magazines, piles of clothes, a layer of dust over everything. And there was no one on the couch except for a couple cushions that Bethany was talking to.

Maybe he was in the bathroom or something. Maybe the guy was really laid back, and that's why he hadn't said anything about the mess.

Bethany soon came back and shook her head. "He says he's feeling a little tired," she told her. "I'll let him rest. I kept him up most of last night."

That made Thea frown even more. "Bethany, no one was in there," she said.

"What? Oh...he's...in the bedroom. He must have gotten up and went upstairs to give us some privacy."

"You just said he was in the living room, and you stood at the couch talking to yourself. Are you okay?"

"He *was* on the couch, but he moved when he heard you at the door. He must not be feeling well," Bethany explained. "Also, I was talking to him from down the hall. I'm sorry that you couldn't meet him."

None of that made any sense, but Thea didn't feel like arguing about the point with her. She took another look around the apartment. Thea wasn't the cleanest person in the world either. With kids and a full-time job, she really couldn't be, but she kept expecting cockroaches to pop up from the mess.

"You've really let this place go, didn't you?"

Bethany's shoulders dropped, and she gave her a look. "I did not let this place go," she told her. "We just finished moving everything of his in, and I'm still trying to get it organized. Did you come here just to question and criticize me?"

Thea quickly shook her head. She didn't want an argument. "No, no. I didn't. I wanted to make sure everything was okay. I was just a little worried about you. You've been missing for the past month."

Bethany shrugged her shoulder. "I found someone who makes me happy and is taking up most of my time. I've been working less, going out more; I'm having a great time. I thought you'd be happy for me."

Thea tried to smile. "I am happy for you," she said softly.

She looked around the kitchen. Something wasn't right. Bethany couldn't be so lost in her own world that she couldn't see that her apartment was a mess, could she? Maybe she needed help.

"It's just his things. It's not like it's garbage," Bethany snapped.

Thea sighed softly and shook her head. "I...you're right. You're right. Not garbage," she muttered. But that was a bold-faced lie. There was garbage everywhere, rotten food, piles and piles of old newspapers. Something was wrong. "But maybe I can help you clean up some? Help organize. You know how much fun we always have when we do it together."

Bethany shook her head. "No, I think I've got it," she promised. She looked back into the living room and sighed. "I should really get back to fixing up the place. I don't want to lose the energy to do it. How about we set up a date to hang out next week, and you and I will have a girl's night out."

Thea didn't want to go. She was sure her friend needed more help than she was letting on. She nodded though and stood up.

"You better call me, or the next time I show up, I won't be knocking, and I'll make sure you two are in the middle of sex."

Bethany rolled her eyes. "If that's what you want to see, then that's what you want to see," she chuckled. "Don't expect me to apologize."

The door slammed shut in front of Thea's face.

Thea stared at the door to her friend's apartment for a while before she decided to walk away. The meeting had left her with a sour taste in her mouth, and she couldn't shake it away. Nothing seemed right. Nothing was right.

Was it the fact that Bethany got a new boyfriend that changed her? That made her delusional? She had boyfriends before, but she never shut her out like this. If it was, then it was ultimately her fault for it. She was the one who pushed the Silver Lining lens on her. And now, she finally found a man who would help her distract herself from work, from her friends, from everything. Show her how special she was. Thea never expected it to get as bad as it did.

But it was clear that, not only did Bethany not want to talk about the mess, she didn't even see the mess. She was happy. Genuinely happy. What position was she in to tell her that she needed to pull it together and get her shit back in order?

She sighed softly and continued walking home. She looked around her and noticed that others were walking alone also but talking to themselves. Or more, talking to someone who clearly wasn't there. Yes, wireless headsets existed, but some of them clearly weren't wearing them. It seemed like everyone was going insane, just like Bethany had.

As she jogged up the steps to her house, she couldn't stop thinking about Bethany. Was she really happy? Did she actually find her happily ever after Prince Charming? Maybe when someone was so deliriously in love, worrying about mess was no longer a thing.

But when Thea and Nathanael had gone through that phase, the worst thing that happened was a few outings that lasted way longer than they anticipated, and Thea going to work with a hangover. But that all fizzled out eventually.

She heard her kids scream as soon as she walked through the door, running down the hall, and almost bowling her over right at the doorway. They were quickly followed by her husband, Nathanael, who was making obscene dinosaur noises. She shook her head fondly.

"Mom's home," she called to everyone before heading to the kitchen.

Her smile dropped as soon as she saw the dirty dishes in the sink. She felt Nathanael's arms slide around her middle, and she slumped back against him.

"Why didn't you do the dishes?" She sighed.

"I was busy entertaining the kids. You know how they get if I don't tire them out," he said quietly. He kissed her neck before resting his chin on her shoulder. "What do you want? Happy kids or clean dishes?"

"Both." She sighed as she pulled away from him. "And you know that the kids shouldn't be running around and screaming like that. The neighbors already complained once about them. I don't want to hear it again. I don't need cops knocking on our door in the middle of the night again."

"Again, I was just trying to keep them happy." He sighed softly. He leaned his head against the table and watched her as she started the dishes. "I did tell them to be quiet though, if that's any consolation."

She looked over her shoulder and gave him a look.

"It usually works better if you aren't chasing them like some monster," she told him. She turned back to the dishes and picked up the pan. "Did the kids eat anything at least?"

"No," he said, looking back towards where they were playing. "I put their plates in the fridge though, so we can just heat them up when they're hungry."

Thea closed her eyes and took in a deep breath. She didn't know what was wrong with Bethany, but everything after seeing her had set Thea on edge. She wasn't sure if she was upset that her friend was living like she was and ignoring her, or if there was something else clearly wrong that Bethany couldn't see.

Or maybe Thea was jealous because Bethany was so happy. She couldn't remember the last time she felt butterflies in her stomach or tingles on her skin from her husband.

It wasn't that Thea wasn't happy. She really was. She had an amazing husband and two great kids. She looked at the dish she was scrubbing clean and sighed. She pushed it into the water-filled sink before turning to look at Nathanael.

"You should be doing this," she told him.

She was sick of feeling like she was the only responsible one out of everyone around her. Her kids saw her as the boring one who always told them to brush their teeth and do their homework while their dad was the fun one. Thea saw her friend for the first time in a long time, and her first thought was the mess in her house.

What was wrong with her?

He raised an eyebrow. "What?"

"You should be cleaning your dishes. Not me," she said as she grabbed the dish towel.

She dried her hands before walking over to him and pushing it against his chest.

He frowned and grabbed the towel before she could drop it. "I never said that you had to clean them. I just hadn't gotten to them yet," he told her. He watched her walk into the living room. "Are you okay? Seems like something's bothering you."

"I'm fine," she muttered.

He shook his head and followed after her. He looked at the kids.

"Go to your room," he told them.

"But Dad..."

"I'm serious." He glared at them, and they jumped up and hurried off to their room. "What's wrong?" he asked again. "Did your visit with Bethany not go well?"

"It went fine," she lied. She sat on the couch and started searching for the remote. When she couldn't find it, she let out a frustrated growl. "Fuck me," she practically yelled.

Nathanael held up his hand and grabbed the remote from the floor. "Seriously, what's wrong?" he asked as he held it out to her.

She snatched it from him and turned on the television. "I just want you to do more to help around the house," she told him.

"Is that it?" he asked carefully, walking on eggshells.

She nodded. "Yeah, that's all I want," she whispered.

He smiled and leaned down to give her a kiss. "I'll do the dishes, and then I'll get the kids to eat. You sit back and relax. Okay?"

He gave her another kiss before he headed back into the kitchen. She sighed and settled back into the couch as she watched her show. She had her Prince Charming. She was sure of it.

But then a commercial for the Silver Lining lens came on. She glanced towards the kitchen and saw her husband struggling in front of the sink. Her chest tightened at the thought, but she couldn't help but wonder if he was the right one for her after all.

What if there was someone better for her out there?

She closed her eyes and forced herself to think of anything else. She was happily married with a great family. There wasn't anything else she needed. She was fine where she was. She loved Nathanael. That was that.

"By the way, my sister agreed to take the kids next Wednesday. We can go to that concert you wanted, and then we can have a nice dinner after. Just you and me. Sound good?" Nathanael said, coming over to her after he'd finished the dishes.

She opened her eyes and looked at him, shrugging sheepishly. She sighed and gave up trying to hide her real problem from him.

"I'm sorry for snapping at you. I'm just tired, and Bethany... she, apparently, is seeing someone, some guy, but all I saw was her talking to an empty couch. And her apartment is a mess, but she doesn't seem to care. It's not like her at all. And she said she'd call after things settled down, but I'm not sure she will because we haven't talked in over a month. I'm worried she won't talk to me ever again. I'm worried that something's going on with her that I can't do anything about." It all just came out in one long rush of stress.

Nathanael sighed. "I'm sorry, honey. You can check up on her more often if you want. I can take the kids for a while now that my work has calmed down a bit."

"You don't think I'm freaking out too much?"

"She's your friend. And if you're worried, then something is definitely wrong. You're not the type to make problems out of nothing. And she *is* your closest friend."

Nathanael sat down next to her and pulled her into a hug. Thea allowed herself to melt into his embrace and took a few deep breaths.

"I'm sorry I snapped at you," she mumbled into his shirt.

"I don't need an apology. I'm just glad you told me what was bothering you. And hey, we got the kids to settle down. We can have dinner, and I am sure they'll come out and eat too if we do. I made your favorite: creamy gnocchi with spinach and spicy sausages."

Thea smiled. This was why she didn't need Prince Charming. Sure, things weren't perfect with her and Nathanael, but she wasn't sure perfect existed anyway. And she had the support of the person she chose to share her life with, so she didn't need anything or anyone else.

And plus, he'd finished the dishes.

Chapter Eight

The Unexpected Truth

Dixon Reid came home from work and dropped his bag off at the door. He and Jade had been together for almost half a year already, and he had never been so happy in his life. Everything good in his life had followed behind her, and he couldn't help but think that she was his good luck charm.

"Babe," he called.

He pulled the mail out from under his arm and started sorting through them before dropping some onto the small stand by the door. They were all bills. Something he would have to deal with later.

They fell on top of another stack of the other bills he had yet to take care of. He frowned at them. Most of them were marked as *past due* or *urgent*. But then he heard Jade's faint voice, and all the thoughts of bills soon vanished from his mind.

"In the kitchen," Jade called.

Dixon walked in to see her dancing around the kitchen while making herself some tea. When she heard him step inside the kitchen, she spun around and grinned at him.

"Oh...someone looks happy."

He laughed quietly and shook his head. "I think they might be extending my contract," he told her. "I heard my producer saying something to someone else while in the break room, and I heard my name. I honestly think that it could be happening."

She squealed and ran over to him. She flung her arms around him and hugged him as tightly as she could.

"Oh, Dixon. I can't believe it. I knew things would turn around for you. I knew you could do it. I'm so happy for you," she whispered.

He pulled her close and lifted her off the floor as he kissed her. He spun them slowly around the kitchen, letting everything he felt inside him flow into the kiss.

Even half a year later, their relationship still made his heart flutter. He had expected the sparks between them to settle down by this point, but their love only grew stronger.

When he finally set her down, her cheeks were flushed, and her eyes shined. It only made him want to kiss her again.

It took every ounce of willpower he had left in him not to though. Instead, he took her hand and pulled it to his lips.

"I think it's cause for celebration. Don't you?"

He was thinking of having a quiet night in. Something that would just let them be together without worrying about anyone else around them.

Waiters had gotten really rude lately, especially to Jade. The last one bumped straight into her without even an apology.

A slow grin spread across her face, and she nodded quickly.

"Oh, I do believe you're right," she said. She bit her bottom lip as she looked around the kitchen. An idea dawned on her, and she looked back to him. "How about we get into something more comfortable, order some takeout, snuggle up on the couch, and watch a movie you love?" she suggested.

"It's like you read my mind," he whispered. He leaned down and kissed her again. His lips tingled as he pulled away. "I'll order the food; you go get changed."

They both jumped when the kettle started whistling. She laughed and put a hand to her heart.

"I forgot about that," she said quietly.

He walked over and took it off the burner. "I'll make this for you too," he assured her. "Go change. I'll bring this in when it's ready."

She pecked his cheek as she passed him. "You're amazing," she called to him.

Dixon grinned and shook his head. Sure, he was amazing, but he wasn't anything compared to her.

As he prepared the tea, he called in to their favorite Chinese place and ordered what they usually got: sweet and sour chicken for her and beef and broccoli for himself.

When he was done with both things, he brought the mug into the bedroom with him.

"The food should be here in about twenty minutes," he told her, setting the mug on the nightstand next to several other untouched mugs. He walked over to her and bent down to give her a quick kiss. "Thank you for doing this. I know you would probably rather go out and have a night of it, but..."

She kissed him quickly and shook her head. "I'm totally fine with a night in," she promised him, not letting him get another word in. She hit him with her pajama top before pulling it on. "Now, change out of those stuffy clothes. I want to start watching movies."

His heart filled his chest to the point where it felt like nothing else would be able to snap him out of his love daze. Her love made him feel like a totally different person.

She made him a different person. A better person. He knew that, without her, he would still be living in the small apartment with nothing to do but watch shit TV and work, living a truly depressing lifestyle like he always feared.

As soon as he finished changing, she walked up behind him and wrapped her arms around him. She buried her face in his back and closed her eyes.

"Congratulations," she whispered, squeezing him around his middle.

He swallowed hard and turned in her arms. He picked her up, and she wrapped her legs around his waist. He kissed her, moving his hand underneath her thin pajama top. Her smooth warm skin sent a shiver through him, and he couldn't stop himself from smiling against her lips.

She pulled away a few moments later, her hair falling around her face as she looked down at him. She gently rubbed her thumb across his cheek, shaking her head slightly.

"We have food coming in twenty minutes," she reminded him.

He smirked and started walking her to the bed. "I think I can make that work," he told her as he dropped onto the bed with her in his lap.

She squeaked before giggling and kissing him again.

"Hm, I think it's fifteen minutes now," she mused.

"I like a challenge," he purred.

He turned them around so she was lying on her back. He grinned down at her before pressing her into the mattress and kissing her.

Just as the doorbell rang for their food, Dixon was carrying Jade out to the couch. He set her down on the sofa and kissed her again.

"I'll be right back," he whispered before winking at her.

The delivery guy had a frown on his face, but accepted the cash and the tip anyway. Dixon frowned at his wallet; he better go to the ATM tomorrow.

He came back with the containers of food.

"This place smells more and more delicious every time we get them," he mused as he fell into the spot next to her. He opened the bag and handed her everything he ordered for her. "And it keeps getting better too."

She laughed softly and shook her head. "It's like they got a newer, better cook," she agreed. She leaned back and turned on the television. "So, what are we watching?" she asked.

"Oh, I heard about this movie with robots taking over the world," he told her as he took the remote. "It's supposed to be really good too. You think you can handle that?" He looked at her and winked.

She stared at him with her eggroll hanging from her mouth. She shoved the rest in quickly before nodding.

"You know I'm always down for a good robot movie," she reminded him. "Makes me feel at home."

He rolled his eyes and playfully pushed her. When she nearly dropped her food, he laughed more.

"Oops." He chuckled. He pulled her back up before kissing her cheek. "I wish you would stop comparing yourself to a robot. It makes me a little upset. I love you so much. Even if you were a robot, you would still be my world."

Jade smiled at him as her eyes softened. She leaned her head on his shoulder just so she could be closer to him.

"I love you too," she reminded him. "With everything I've got."

"I know you do," he whispered.

He turned and kissed her forehead gently. He gave himself a second to just be with her before turning back to the television. He found the movie he was looking for and clicked on it.

"I really hope you like this," he told her.

She snuggled up against his side as she started eating again.

"I promise that I will," she assured him.

He grinned and kissed her forehead before he picked up his own container. He settled in to watch the movie, but he couldn't stop thinking about how amazing his life was in that moment.

"You know, Jade," he said after a while. "I think I have to tell you something."

They had long finished their food and were just holding each other. She was tucked against his chest, and he had his arms wrapped securely around her.

She tilted her head back slightly to show him that she was listening.

"I love you, so fucking much that it hurts," he whispered. He looked down at her, rubbing a hand over her stomach. He buried his nose into her hair. "And I know this is probably the wrong time to say this, but I'm so scared of losing you. And if I do ever lose you, I'm afraid that I will never be able to come back from it. I would never be able to love anyone else as much as I love you."

Jade shifted until she was facing him and sitting on his lap. She took his face in her hands and tilted it a little more.

"I love you, Dixon," she whispered before kissing his forehead. "I will always love you." She kissed his nose. "And I promise that I will *never* leave you unless you want me to."

She kissed his lips gently.

His heart hammered in his chest as she kissed him. He grabbed the bottom of her shirt and let his fingers hang from it.

"I would never want you to leave. You're my world," he told her.

It was the truth. He couldn't see any part of his future without her right in the center.

She smiled and pressed their foreheads together. "Then I'll never leave you. I promise."

* * *

It was raining one Saturday afternoon, and the sidewalk was filled with puddles. Neither Dixon nor Jade cared about any of that though. They were simply happy to be in each other's presence.

They were supposed to be in a restaurant for their one-year anniversary dinner, but there was a mix-up in their reservation with another couple's, and they had to wait an hour before another table cleared. Dixon was going to suggest they just head home, where he would make them both dinner.

However, Jade decided that that wasn't how the night was supposed to go. She told him to follow her, and they left the restaurant.

She pulled him around the city until she stopped them at a Mexican food truck, and they both ordered the messiest and largest burrito on the menu.

After they ate, they started their walk in the rain. They were already drenched. Dixon pointed out, what was a little more water going to do to them? Plus, she looked beautiful whenever she laughed with strands of hair sticking to her face.

It wasn't the night he planned, but it turned out to be more than perfect, mostly because he was with her. He pulled her closer as they walked, lifting her up easily as they passed a puddle so she wouldn't have to step in it and dirty her shoes. It was just so easy being with her.

She giggled, hitting his chest. "I'm already soaked," she told him. "You don't need to keep doing that."

"I know," he told her. "I just love having you close."

He kissed her cheek before setting her back down. He looked around and noticed that they were near the park. There weren't many people hanging around like there usually was because of the rain.

It's now or never, he thought as he took her hand.

He pulled her to a stop and grinned when she turned to face him. He pulled her hand to his lips before kissing her fingers and getting down on one knee.

"Jade," he started as he rooted around the pockets of his jacket for a tiny red velvet box. "I was planning to do this by a nice candlelit dinner while we were both dry, but I think here is just as perfect. Because I will love you anywhere and any way you want me to. I can't imagine a life without you."

Suddenly, someone knocked hard into him and sent him to the ground. The ring fell out of his pocket along with his car keys, where the Silver Lining remote was attached.

Shocks wracked the right side of his head, causing his eye to start twitching, and his head to jerk to the side. He pushed himself up and quickly swiped his keys and the ring out of the water. He pressed a hand to his temple as pain formed a band around his head.

"I'm okay," he murmured, reaching up a hand towards Jade.

He expected her to grab hold of it, ask him if he was okay, maybe press a kiss to his temple like she always did when he was in pain, but he was met with nothing. He turned and looked up, desperately searching for his soulmate.

"Jade?" he asked, pushing himself to his feet.

He looked around but didn't see any sign of her.

His vision started to flicker as he looked around, and the pain in his head only got worse. Everything around him seemed to be skewing sideways and flickering in and out. The lights grew dimmer, and the rain beat harder against the sidewalk, making his head pound even more.

He squeezed his eyes shut and tried to get it to stop, but nothing was working.

"Jade!" he yelled.

He lifted his head and tried desperately to find where she had run off to. He blinked a few times as his vision went out of focus. His eyes squeezed shut again, and he counted down from ten before opening them again.

People surrounded him, all walking like they couldn't see anyone else but the person standing next to them. The problem was, no one was standing next to them. They were all walking alone and talking to thin air.

He shook his head and looked down at his remote. He hit it a few times, and Jade blinked into life for a split second before disappearing again.

"No," he whispered as he tried hitting the button one more time.

When she popped up again, she wasn't all there and quickly vanished after only a few seconds.

"No!" He hit the remote hard against his hand, but it flew out of his wet fingers and skidded across the ground.

He dove for it and scrambled to his knees once he had it. He froze when he saw his reflection in a puddle. His face was hollow, and his hair looked thin and moments away from falling out. He placed a hand over his face, feeling how rough his skin was.

He looked up again at everyone who passed him. They all looked as sickly pale and thin as he did. Like they hadn't taken care of themselves in months. He pushed himself up and grabbed a hold of someone's elbow.

"Do you know what happened?" he asked the man desperately.

However, he was willfully ignored. The man just kept walking, talking with his imaginary companion, almost like Dixon wasn't even there, almost like he didn't even see him.

Dixon let his hand drop, and he looked around. Not a single person was paying attention to him. He walked a little further before someone bumped into him, and he nearly fell again. He shook his head as tears started to fall down his face. He clicked the button over and over and over again, but Jade never came back.

He fell back against the stone wall of a nearby building and closed his eyes.

"Please," he whispered, feeling the words echo against the hole inside his chest. "I just want Jade back. Please. I don't want to be alone again."

He slid to the ground, still pressing the button.

The rain kept pouring down, and the people kept walking, lost in their own worlds. Dixon desperately tried to join them.

Dixon eventually found his way home. His house was a mess. Cooking for a person that wasn't actually there meant a lot of food just sat there, going to waste and stinking up the place. Dixon hit the lights, then hit them again. He realized he hadn't paid the electric bill.

Wait, did he still have a career? He couldn't remember the last time he picked up his guitar.

He couldn't destroy his house any more than it already was, and he was pretty sure he had no alcohol left, so he couldn't do the same thing he'd done after the last fight with Zoe.

Instead, he peeled off his wet clothes and settled for cracking open all of the windows and cleaning up a little bit while he thought about what had happened.

Jade wasn't real. The lens didn't give him a real person, he knew this now. But when he met her, she had seemed so... *extraordinary*. And she felt so real. She felt like the realest thing in existence.

And yet, now he was alone. He had always been alone. His mind just conjured up the perfect woman without a woman actually being there.

No wonder he'd thought she was too good to be true. She never complained, always wanted to do what he did, laughed at all his jokes, and had interests but was always more interested to hear about his day.

And she was always there. A lot more than anyone should be, really. If someone had asked him to be that devoted, he'd strongly object. What did that say about him when it came to his thoughts, that the perfect partner wouldn't be all that perfect unless they were from a lens, a fake?

A few hours after the pain in his head returned, and the world around him shifted again, he watched glumly, a soggy dish in his hand as Jade materialized next to him.

His brain needed a moment to decide if she was supposed to be wearing the soaked clothes she had been wearing on the street, before changing her into a dry set. That made him keep his cool a bit better.

"Dixon! Oh my god, are you okay?" Jade wrapped her arms around him.

He felt the warmth emanate from her.

He wanted to smile at her and forget he had ever seen anything. Just slide right back into the lie of their relationship and not think about it.

But he remembered the reflection he had seen in his bathroom mirror, when he'd taken a break from cleaning to take a leak, and ended up staring at himself for half an hour.

Instead, he grabbed her hands and pulled them away from his body. She looked at him with a frown. She was beautiful.

"You're not real," he said.

Maybe if he said it enough, his brain would register it and understand.

"What? Of course, I am." She lifted one of her arms. "You can touch me, see me, hear me, smell me, taste me." She smirked. "How does that not make me real?"

"If I turn off the lens, you vanish. No one else can see you."

God, it was hard to remember that.

"So? I still make you happy. Don't I?" Jade tried to get closer to him.

"No, you don't. Not when I'm in my right mind. I mean, look at me!"

"You look very handsome," she said.

That was what she'd always said when he'd asked her. At least Zoe had been blunt about it, been honest with him, and told him straight up when he looked like shit.

Right now, he would prefer that response. This one felt empty and shallow, almost forced.

He laughed. "Now I know why Zoe left. She was right. I was going through the motions. That's all I've ever done with you. I've lost everything."

He stomped to the living room and grabbed the remote.

"Dixon…"

"No." He pressed the button.

Nothing happened.

"Dixon, let's talk," Jade insisted.

"I said, no," Dixon repeated as he pressed the button again.

Still nothing.

Jade looked at him with tears in her eyes. It was only after several more tries, did he realize he couldn't turn her off. The remote must have glitched from the rain or the fall. Or the technology was fallible.

That wasn't surprising right now.

"I don't want to see you. Don't follow me into the bedroom."

"It's my bedroom too."

Her voice was flat. Zoe would have roared at him in anger, fought for her opinion. She was real, a real woman he loved that everyone could see. He'd always thought he caved under her strength too much, but when he looked at the woman his brain conjured, this woman who did everything he wanted and never asked him for anything in return… he felt ashamed.

"Do you even need sleep? Your part of the closet is completely empty. I looked at it. There's nothing there. If you don't need clothes, you don't need food…"

"I don't need sleep," Jade finished.

"Then you can stay in the living room. Or even better, leave."

"I can't. I can't leave if you don't."

"And then you ask me how I can say you're not real," Dixon said. "I need a real person in my life. Hell, Zoe and I argued all the time, but I'd prefer that over this…this… façade."

He ignored the tears and decided to spend the rest of the day in his bedroom. He'd cleaned up a lot in there. Not that he could see it now. The apartment looked the same as always, cheery and comfy.

He called his producer; he didn't pick up. Dixon found himself dismissing it as he caught notice of what he was doing. He didn't need to call anyone; he just needed a distraction from the hell of his reality. The lens didn't just create Jade; it altered his outlook completely, and he had to actively fight against his brain to remember the truth.

He spent the night doing just that, recalling his own face in the mirror every time he needed to. Reaching into her half of the closet helped too. Now that he could see it, the clothes shifted, and the closet sometimes looked empty.

He had no idea what to do. Maybe he could call the clinic and have them remove the lens? Dixon used the last of the battery on his phone to call the place he'd gotten the lens from. No one answered. Then his phone died.

He really needed to try and pay the electric bill tomorrow.

***

"I'm sorry, but the lens has been attached to your brain for too long; it's too fused to your receptors to remove it. You could lose your eye. You said the remote broke?"

The doctor, a different one this time, wrote down a note. Why? He didn't know. The clinic he had gotten the lens from had apparently closed. He'd driven all around town, looking for an open one, and this was the only one he found still in business.

"My Zeta flickers in and out randomly. It's disorienting. Can't you just turn it off? And have it stay off?" Dixon asked.

"Please, honey, talk to me. I love you, remember?" Jade was right at the edge of his vision.

Dixon tried to tune her out. He especially tried to tune out how her hand rubbed over the very big bump on her stomach.

She'd gotten pregnant before this whole debacle started. They were so excited to start a family together that he impregnated her in hopes of having a daughter and naming her Arabella, after his great-grandmother.

Little did he know, impregnating a Zeta was literally impossible. His imagery of her pregnancy was simply a result of the lens causing him to see what he wanted to see rather than what was real.

The lens gave him what his brain thought was perfect. But his brain didn't just use his desires; it used his conjectures, his trauma, his assumptions and prejudices, and the expectations of others. Everything that went into what he was looking for in a relationship and how he acted around his Zeta.

He finally had the chance to be with his dream girl, and all he wanted was out.

"Please, I don't want to see her anymore. Please make it stop. Make her go away."

"I don't know if I even have the right tools to do so. The lenses have been discontinued for months now due to the side effects. But I can try and find some. It's an old model; the company cycled through several different versions of the lens over the past few months. It's going to take a while. Especially since you are the first one who has ever asked for it to be removed," the doctor paused, "Are you sure..."

"Yes. I'll pay again if I have to, since my 30-day trial is over. I want to go back to normal. If you can't remove it, just turn it off permanently."

"We can try and sever the connection between your brain and the lens. It'll hurt. We'll also need to try and find a surgeon who's qualified to do something like this before we can schedule anything."

"I don't care."

"You don't mean that. I know you don't mean that. Dixon, honey, we can be happy if you just let yourself be with me. Please be with me and our baby. We can start that family we've always talked about. We can finally be happy. Please stop fighting this; we're perfect together." Jade barely stopped to take a breath as she trailed behind him, waddling under the weight of her belly.

She wasn't real. None of it was real.

Dixon left the office and went to his car. He'd been living out of it for the past few weeks. He could lock Jade out and not listen as she pleaded for him to reconsider. He crawled in the back seat and shut his eyes as he tried to tune out Jade's pleading.

He should have tried to get Zoe back. Or stayed alone and killed himself by drinking.

Anything was better than this nightmare he was now living in.

Chapter Nine

I Will Never Leave You

Bethany settled against Haven's chest as they watched a movie together. It was a quiet and rainy Sunday morning, and they had nothing better to do all day.

A lot had happened since he moved in with her. He lost his job but promised to find another one. Though she didn't care. She was just happy to have him around their apartment more. She loved waking up to him, coming home to him after work, and seeing him every chance she got.

Thea never visited them again. It was for the best. Bethany didn't like how Thea judged her apartment and her relationship. Even after Bethany tried to explain to her that they were moving in together, and of course, things were going to be messy for a bit, Thea still thought something was wrong and tried to meddle into her life.

Bethany didn't care what anyone thought. She had done what Thea told her to do and fell in love with someone. If she didn't like it now, then it's on her.

At the thought, she turned more into Haven and pressed her face into his neck.

This is nice," she told him quietly. She looked up, just in time to see him looking at her, a smile on his face.

Haven ran a warm hand over her back in a rhythmic motion, calming her down.

"It really is," he whispered, brushing his hair back from his forehead. "You make me so happy. Did you know that?"

"I did." She grinned, trying to nuzzle closer to him, even though she was almost on top of him. She closed her eyes and let out a small sigh. "My entire life changed when I met you."

"You mean when you got the lens put in," he teased.

She sat up and looked at him. "Well... yeah, but that's only the start of it. Even if I shut it off, nothing would change."

She had finally found her perfect partner, and nothing could ruin it.

"You think so?" he asked, tilting his head to the side.

He reached up and gently ran his thumb under the eye with the lens.

She leaned into his touch and closed her eyes again.

"I really do," she whispered. She pulled back slightly before looking at him. "I'm going to prove it to you."

He sighed and shook his head. "You don't have to prove anything, Bethany," he told her.

"Oh no, I'm going to prove it to you," she said as she climbed out of his lap.

She'd even prove it to the little voice in her head that said this was too perfect to be real. She found the remote in one of her jackets draped over the couch and pulled it out. She held the remote and pressed the button.

The air left her lungs when Haven vanished from the couch.

"Haven?"

She looked around the apartment, trying to see if he walked away somewhere, in an attempt at a joke. That was when she noticed the world around her had completely shifted. She noticed that nothing in her home was how it was just seconds before.

Trash littered the floor. Rotten food, forgotten bags filled with garbage, clothes strewn about, some even covered with substances she couldn't identify. There were bugs crawling all over the walls and on the half-empty plates thrown all over the floor and sink. The window she had imagined as open was actually broken and shattered, and there was a foul odor coming from somewhere inside the apartment.

The worst part, she wasn't sure if it was the result of the rotting food, or if an animal had somehow crawled inside, died, and rotted.

She covered her mouth quickly and spun around, seeing more and more garbage and forgotten food lying about. She felt like she was going to be sick to her stomach just at the sight of it. A rat hurried along in her line of view. She jumped and turned around again. The television wasn't on. It looked like it would never be on again, with the crack on its screen.

As quickly as she could, she pressed the button to turn on the lens again, vowing not to close her eyes this time. Everything flickered along with the shock in her head, before turning back into the perfect world that it had been before. Haven was back on the couch, in the one spot free of debris.

Haven looked at her with a soft look. "I told you that you didn't have to do that," he told her.

He stood up and walked over to her gently, pulling her against his chest.

She choked on a sob and pressed her face into his body.

"It's everywhere," she cried, her body shaking. "I...how come I can't see it?"

He shushed her gently, kissing the top of her head. "You'll forget soon. Don't worry. Just don't shut it off, and you won't have to worry about it. I promise."

She clung onto him until the images of her decaying apartment and the smell of it left her. She pulled back and smiled up at him.

"What are we doing standing here?" she asked. "I thought we were watching a movie."

"You're right; we were," he said softly. He sat down and pulled her against his chest again. He kissed her head and slowly took out the remote. "I love you."

Bethany tilted her head back and looked up at him.

"I love you too," she whispered.

She settled back against him. She was happy and safe. Nothing else mattered.

* * *

Bethany wasn't safe though. She thought it would be easy to just forget, to just immerse herself in the fantasy world and ignore the real world, because it's not like she was happy in it anyway. But the façade kept falling apart.

Haven didn't have a job, so he was around her all the time. She needed space, needed to breathe, needed somebody she didn't have to babysit or take care of.

And then when he did get a job, she wanted him back in the apartment, back in her life all the time, because they no longer spent any time together. So, he got a part-time job as a waiter, but part of her knew that wasn't real. She didn't know what she wanted anymore.

And then when he was at home all the time again, the cycle started all over. And he never called her out on it, just bent to her will. And the more he did, the more the logical part of her brain piped up, saying that this couldn't be real. She was living in some sort of love-sick nightmare.

"Honey, please stop pushing me away." Haven looked up at her from the couch. "Let me say this, no matter how much you try and push me away, I will never leave. You can't argue your way out of this relationship by nitpicking at me. I love you too much for that."

"But that isn't healthy! You need to be your own person, not let me walk all over you!" Bethany finally screamed.

She heard a thump somewhere in the background, but when she tried to focus on it, she couldn't register where it had come from. Bethany looked around herself, and her eyes fell on the remote. She walked over.

"Please, don't hurt yourself with that anymore. You know how you feel when you turn it off," Haven said.

She glared at him and clicked the button. The smell hit her nostrils, and Bethany screamed, trying to get the crawling bugs off her skin. She needed to turn on the lens again; she couldn't live like this.

"Miss, open the door," someone banged on the entrance to her apartment.

"Shit."

A heavy thump sounded, and a man shoulder-pounded against the door so hard that the lock broke. Bethany clicked the remote on instinct.

She managed to register the police uniform right before her world shifted, and Haven returned. Then, she saw nothing but him, sitting in the middle of the couch, smiling as the sunlight streamed through the open windows.

"What's wrong with me?" Bethany asked.

She could feel a pressure on her arms, but she had no idea why.

"Relax, honey, you're okay." Haven got up and hugged her. His fingers carded through her hair.

"I'm still mad at you."

"I know, but everything will be fine. You'll see."

"Miss, miss, can you hear me?"

***

Bethany woke up in an empty room the next morning and immediately started panicking.

"Honey, why are you upset?" Haven knelt in front of her, soft smile in place, wearing the black shirt Bethany had once told him brought out the mystery in his eyes.

"Shut up. Just shut up!" Bethany closed her eyes.

Maybe if she did, he'd stop talking. And touching her, trying to pull her into a hug and comfort her. She didn't want that; she didn't want to calm down. She felt that was a bad thing.

She knew she had to find the remote for some reason. She couldn't really remember why, but she knew it was important. She crawled away from him and patted around. But there was no furniture in the apartment, nor clothes. Nothing. She had no idea why.

"Please, don't," Haven pleaded. "Please don't run away from me; we can be happy together, like always, like we always promised each other, if you just stop fighting with me."

She couldn't find the remote; she couldn't find anything.

The door opened, and a woman in a nurse's uniform came into the room.

"Bethany, dear, calm down, okay?" The nurse stopped a few steps away, making sure she looked as unthreatening as possible.

"Make him leave, make him leave," Bethany chanted.

"It's okay; we'll make him leave," the nurse pulled out a needle. "This will help."

Chapter Ten

The Downfall of Society

Bethany wasn't answering her phone no matter how much Thea called.

"I should just show up at her door and make a scene. Force her to listen to me."

"That will just push her away, won't it?" Nathanael asked.

He'd just come home from a night shift at work. Thea was grateful that he stayed up to listen to her even though he was obviously extremely tired. He truly was the best husband in the world.

"So, what do I do? I can't just let her go. There's rotten food inside her apartment. The last time I was there, I'm pretty sure I saw a rat in the corner. Who knows what she'll catch if I just leave her there?" Thea slumped down on the bed next to her husband. "She helped me so much during the worst years of my life. It's time to return the favor. I can't just abandon my friend."

"Why don't I research the lens more? Just to make sure that wasn't the reason why this all happened? You said she's not normally like this, so there must be something going on that came into her life recently," he chimed in. "You can call that coworker of hers that you know, Natalie, remember her? Maybe you can find out the name of the dude."

"Good idea, honey." Thea jumped up and pulled her datebook out of her purse.

She knew she had that phone number written down somewhere.

After several rings, a woman answered the phone, and Thea could hear a lot of noise in the background.

At a lull, Thea piped up. "Hey, Nat, this is Thea. I don't know if you remember me. I'm Bethany's friend?"

"Oh, hey, how's Bethany doing? She hasn't been at work in almost a year." Natalie sounded stressed. "But then again, a lot of people haven't. We've been so swamped, and we lost a bunch of our clients. At this rate, we'll probably have to shut down."

"Shut down? Why? Is there some sort of problem?" Thea asked.

"I have no idea, but a lot of people have been calling out sick lately, some of them just not showing up to work without any notice. I know we're not alone." Natalie sighed. "A lot of businesses are dealing with the same thing; I think it's a health thing, some sort of bug going around or something? I've seen a few of them talk to themselves on the street. They didn't acknowledge me, so I hope whatever it is, it isn't contagious. I outgrew imaginary friends when I was five. I guess some people haven't," Natalie said, directed to probably some of her other coworkers. "I do think it's an eye thing though, if that helps. Maybe some sort of bug blinding them to hallucinate?"

Thea bit her fingernail. "Why do you think that?"

"The coworkers I've seen all have something in their eye."

"A silver glow?"

"Look, I'm sorry, but I have to go. I'm really busy."

"Yeah, okay, thank you for answering."

Thea didn't even register that Natalie had hung up on her without a goodbye. If the lens was the cause of all this, then it was all Thea's fault.

She had been the one to push this "thing" on Bethany.

"Honey?" Nathanael's hands managed to catch Thea before her knees gave out.

She curled around him, incredibly grateful she had him to lean on. "This is all my fault. The lens did it. The lens ruined Bethany's life."

"It's not your fault. You didn't know. You just wanted the best for her, and I'm sure you'll do your best to fix it. I'll help."

He shushed her and held her until she could gather her despair together and turn it into determination.

She would fix this. She could fix this.

* * *

Thea never paid attention before, but soon, she started noticing it more and more after her conversation with Natalie. How many silver eyes were around her. She began paying more attention to them, to strangers on the streets she would've never acknowledged before.

The people who she'd assumed were talking on a wireless headset were actually talking to thin air, hands fluttering around invisible people, holding hands, or petting something in mid-air.

They didn't acknowledge Thea, sometimes even walking through her, pushing her away so strongly that she would stumble onto the ground. Thea would walk along the street and notice how many of the people, whom she thought were homeless, were just normal working-class people like her who had the lens. These people were unkempt, rancid, and gaunt.

The lens didn't just ruin Bethany's life. It looked like half the city was decomposing.

Thea walked around and superimposed Bethany's face on these unfortunate people, and that just made her want to fix this more.

Calling the cops did nothing. Maybe forcing them to deal with her face-to-face would.

"Look, lady, she moved and didn't leave a forwarding address. We can't find her." The cop smacked his gum as he typed on his computer.

He was a man in his thirties but looked incredibly worn down. It made Thea speak softly.

"But she's obviously in danger. At least, if this guy is actually real, he is an abuser who has isolated her from anyone who could help. She hasn't even gone to work," Thea insisted.

"She wouldn't be the only one. Half the city is a mess, people going crazy left and right, ruining everything for the rest of us. We don't have time to investigate every single one of these nutcases. I'll add her to the list, but don't hold your breath."

"Can't you just run a scan on her lens? Isn't there a serial code for each one?" Thea asked.

"What do we look like? The CIA? I barely have enough men to fix my own town, much less yours. But I just sent a report up the chain. Now, we'll see if they'll do anything." The cop gestured for her to leave.

Thea came back home, finally accepting that she would need to do this alone, without any help.

"There are no sources on lens removal anywhere online." Thea thumped her head on the table. She'd been researching this for five hours that day, sitting at the kitchen table in front of her laptop. "But considering this thing melds with the brain, I'm pretty sure there isn't an easy way to do it."

"The site doesn't say anything, but the woman who actually invented the lens lives in New York City," Nathanael chimed in.

Thea was glad that he had taken over when it came to their children so she could dedicate her time to this.

"I need to go to New York then." Thea waited for her husband to object.

He didn't; instead, he nodded. "I can find the address. Just promise me that you'll be careful. I know you've been doing this for a while given that you're a journalist, but you don't know what they've done to keep people quiet over there. Whatever's going on, the epicenter is definitely not the best place to be right now."

Thea nodded. "I promise I'll be careful. And I'll call you when I get there."

* * *

The Silver Lining corporate office refused to let her in when she arrived two days later; the receptionist didn't even let her finish her sentence before security came to drag her away.

But Thea wasn't going to give up that easily. She didn't fly all the way to New York just to walk away after one simple no. She waited at the entrance until a black car pulled up, and Marissa Sinclair, the CEO, walked out.

Thea stopped Marissa from entering the building.

"Ms. Sinclair, may I have a word, please?" Thea managed to blurt the sentence out before shock took over.

The CEO had a lens in her eye. Thea could clearly see the silver glow coming from the eye. That changed her tactic.

"I would like to ask you a question. Well, it's more of a request, really."

"Yes?" Marissa's eyes snagged on the ID badge around Thea's neck, and she quickly moved to the side. "Thea, is it? Come into my office; it's a little more private there."

Thea followed Marissa down the empty lobby and up the stairs, the building echoing with every step. All the lenses on the shelves drew Thea's attention. There were so many of them.

"I noticed there is no prototype here, just *version two.*"

"The prototype is in my own eye." Marissa leaned on her desk. "Can you tell me what you wanted to talk about?"

So, Thea sat down and began her story, starting with Bethany. "My friend, Bethany Rose, has been hurt by love, way too many times. She always assured me that she was done with it, happy with just one-night stands, but I could see the sadness in her eyes. And I wanted to help. So, I introduced her to Silver Lining. A month later, I realized she had gotten the lens and met a man. But when I went over to see her, her apartment was a mess. Rotten food everywhere. I saw her talking to herself. Now, she is missing. She hasn't been to work in almost a year, and I can't find her anywhere. I even tried going to the cops, but they're completely useless. I think there is something wrong with the software of the lens, maybe, because this is happening to so many people."

"So, what do you want *me* to do?" Marissa asked, her tone calm and unemotional.

"I came to you because I think you had good intentions when you created the lens, but you need to fix this. This isn't healthy!"

"How do you know it's the lens that's causing all this?"

"Because nothing else fits. It doesn't make any sense otherwise!"

"I have not been informed of any side effects, but I will look into it." Marissa's eyes looked down at Thea's left hand. "Maybe you just don't know what it's like to finally find someone who is right for you. You have had an easier time with love than most people."

Thea chuckled with no humor. "We all have our issues. But abandoning your entire life because of a man that is not real? It's absurd!"

"How do you know he's not real?"

"Because she was talking to thin air." Thea paused. "Is your Zeta real?"

"As real as he can be."

That wasn't a straight answer. "Where is he now?"

Marissa shrugged. "I don't know, exactly, but maybe work? Blaise doesn't work with me. And I don't need to account for all of his movements." Marissa got up. "But I will make sure that I check up on the issues you have brought to my attention. But I don't think things are that dire. At least, not as dire as the loneliness otherwise. I don't think that is something you can understand."

Marissa gestured at Thea's left hand. "I wanted to help the people like me, the ones who thought they were unlovable after many, many failed attempts at finding love, and those who might have left it too early because of it." She spoke with an air of superiority and sounded like she had made so many speeches that she believed her own hype.

"Thank you for looking into it."

Thea got up. She had to leave now because Marissa had nothing to say that would let her dig deeper. And the cool front standing before her gave her an idea of the woman who had created the lens.

It all made sense now.

* * *

A few weeks later, Thea got a phone call from the cop she had filed the missing report with.

"Did you find something?"

"Bethany Rose has been admitted to the psychiatric ward at Stable Memorial Hospital. She was found in an isolated building with several other people, all talking to themselves. She won't be discharged for quite a while, well, not until she stabilizes and regains her sanity. You're free to visit her if you want."

Thea felt her knees buckle. *A psych hospital?* "Thank you for telling me."

"No problem. Take care."

"Bye."

Thea spent the next several hours staring at a wall, then took a train to the hospital as soon as possible.

* * *

Thea tried to publish her story about Bethany, but her newspaper, *The Daily Spill,* was contacted by lawyers immediately after it went out to the public. She had to drop it or lose her job. She couldn't afford that; they had a mortgage to pay, and her husband barely made over minimum wage working as a chef.

"I really hope this works," Thea muttered as she typed up all her suspicions and sent an email to any of her friends who could possibly investigate.

There wasn't much though; anyone who tried to write about this matter was instantly crushed, swiftly and severely. There had to be someone who could do this. But all she got was radio silence.

Every time Thea doubted the validity of her assumptions, and that she was wasting everyone's time, she went and saw Bethany in the ward.

Thea would try and get Bethany's attention over and over. Sometimes Bethany would see her; sometimes she wouldn't.

The doctors tried to ask the Silver Lining company to repair the remote, broken in the scuffle with the police officer, but no one ever answered. The only response had been that any repairs had to be done within thirty days of the lens' installation. Since it's been a year, there was no obligation to fix it anymore.

Thea watched in horror as Bethany tried to ignore the man her brain had conjured with the help of the lens, just before giving in and getting into an argument with him. Eventually, the nurses would have to intervene and put her to sleep so she didn't hurt herself.

If Bethany could see her, Thea would be spending all her time in the room talking to her about anything she could, trying to help her avoid the man, Haven. If Bethany couldn't see Thea, she would be wasting her time staring at the silver eye.

The silver eye she would never be able to forget.

Chapter Eleven

Marissa Sinclair

Marissa thought she was too nihilistic for denial, but as the days went by, she realized she had steeped herself in it.

"I'm not happy."

"What do you mean, love? Don't you think I've made your life better?" Blaise asked, leaning on her office wall.

"As much as you can, I guess." Marissa turned off the lens.

She didn't know why she could do that so easily when everyone else who wore the lens seemed to struggle. Maybe it was because her brain had made the technology. Or because she turned off the lens so often that her eyes became accustomed to it. Or maybe she was just a cold-hearted bitch who didn't deserve love, even a concocted one. She did think Blaise was real as long as the lens was on, but her mind couldn't stop nitpicking every inch of their relationship.

Why did her mind think she needed someone who never accomplished anything, who complimented her constantly, and who stammered every time she asked him something that he wasn't programmed to answer?

Apparently, when she couldn't stand his "romantic mode" anymore, he couldn't think of anything else to do or say, like he didn't know how to live for himself.

"You still talk about him. Say his name in your sleep," Blaise said once, out of the blue.

Marissa wanted to say "Who?" and pretend she didn't know, but she couldn't. She'd actually hired a private detective to find out where Levi had vanished to. A part of her hoped he had gotten the lens also, just so they had something in common.

Which was when she found out he had married the woman he left her for and moved to the outskirts of France. They had a dog and two kids, the perfect life Marissa had always wanted.

She scrolled through his social media once every few months, picking at the scar. She compared Levi's expression to the ones in the photos they had taken together.

She was clearly not over him. Maybe if she didn't pretend to be okay with things or tried to become a different person for him. If she didn't play a part, would he have liked her? Would he have changed himself for her? Supported her? Like he did for the other woman?

Was she even worthy of love?

Her brain didn't seem to think so, if her relationship with Blaise was any indication. Blaise was everything Levi couldn't be for her, but she couldn't help but see Levi's face every time she looked over at her Zeta.

Marissa stared outside her window and down to the empty streets below, to the once-busy streets. Occasionally, she saw a few people wandering around muttering to themselves, but they were usually quickly grabbed and pulled into a car so they didn't cause harm to the rest of the world. Others walked side by side, almost too scared to go out alone as if the lens would suddenly jump up at them from a dark alley.

She used to think loneliness was a curse. But now, she knew it was the fear of loneliness instead. The fear that drove everyone to settle down for someone less than ideal. She had shown people the bad sides of being alone. But this just increased people's desperation.

There wasn't any reason to go out alone anymore. People paired off, warding themselves from spending time with others, and used the story of the lens as a modern nightmare. People who spent their time in a world constructed for them wandered around like wraiths, starving and delusional, as a walking warning against not being complacent, looking for more. People stayed in bad situations even more now, using shitty and abusive relationships as a shield against this living representation of an even worst version of the alternative.

On the opposite end, others bucked both versions of the world and lived life happily while in solitary. Marissa considered them the bravest and had no idea how they functioned.

She pressed a hand against the glass before closing her eyes. She couldn't believe that she had created the world they now lived in, this nightmare of a universe. She couldn't believe that her loneliness had spread to almost every single person in the modern world, debilitating them to their own demise. She was glad there were still countries that had never heard of the lens, though once upon a time, she did hope to spread it to them as well.

Her company now only consisted of a few people in empty offices, people who had nothing else to do or didn't care about the company's sins. And a slew of people in the factories were still producing the lenses, with or without Marissa's consent.

People tried to protest against Silver Lining and shut the whole company down, but she managed to get the courts on her side and moved it to a production in secrecy before the word spread. And then she just purely had no energy left to stop them from turning into a global conglomerate.

Now, she had no control left over the company, giving up her share and acting like just another customer. Satellite offices throughout the country freely did whatever they wanted.

It didn't matter anymore though. The world outside the walls of the psychiatric ward she had checked herself into wasn't one worth living in. Sure, she had a big fancy place, all the money anyone could ask for, and people who pretended to be her friends just to access her wealth.

But what was any of that worth in a world where she couldn't connect to anyone, and a world without the man she truly wanted to be with, Levi?

Not even her own Zeta understood her anymore; he kept asking her why she was in the ward, insisting she was okay and that she should check herself out and get back to her life, trying to bribe her with treats like a child. She wished she still had the option of turning the lens off, but even her own remote eventually broke.

She used to think that she would be able to create something that made everyone happier, less lonely, a creation that would change the world for the better. Prove how fake love was, and how people didn't have to change themselves or work together to be in love. She had no one left who actually cared about her, pushing them all away for a Zeta she no longer wanted.

She squeezed her eyes shut before pushing away from the window.

Her room was small and bare, with two chairs so she could occasionally imagine Blaise sitting with her. When she felt particularly masochistic, she walked outside to see all the other patients walking with their own Zetas. Most of them were so out of touch with reality that they were forced into the hospital against their will so the nurses could watch over them to prevent their inevitable deaths.

She used to pass her time reading letters people wrote to her, soon stopping once she realized they were all either hate mail or threats of death from those who lost someone to the lens.

Sure, she had the option to stop the lens, file a lawsuit and shut everything down, but she couldn't bring herself to do it. It represented a sort of self-flagellation, and she pretty much thought that was the only thing that kept her alive today. Her doctor stopped suggesting alternatives a long time ago.

Her eyes might be busy imagining an entire person, but she could still daydream whenever she wanted. Blaise couldn't interfere with her thoughts and willingly left the room whenever she needed space. Or maybe she made him do it. She had no idea anymore.

Every night, Marissa would sit back on her bed and sink into the what-if scenario that had haunted her since the beginning of her creation. What if she had tried to be honest with Levi from the start? Didn't play the woman who was okay with everything and, instead, made him break up with his side chick for the sake of exclusivity? Or maybe he would have been a one-night stand, and *she'd* rejected *him*, or maybe he would eventually realize that she was perfect for him and stayed with her?

She went with that. She closed her eyes and summoned the story. It would be hard; they would argue a lot, especially because they would have to stay in an apartment close to her school. She would also need a lot of whiteboards, and he would need to make sure he convinced her to eat and drink whenever she got distracted.

But eventually, she would have her degree, and they would be able to move into a bigger house. She would get a job at a university or something doing life-changing research so she could spend more time with him. He would work at any job he wanted because he was more than qualified for anything that crossed his path.

And they would get a dog. An easy breed that she wouldn't have to walk for hours at a time. She would go crazy going through toys and dog food, and asking a thousand questions to the veterinarian, and Levi would stand next to her and smirk at her paranoid madness, but then he would smooth out her approach with his significant charm.

They'd get a house, four bedrooms, two baths, with a pool. They would sit and read, in companionable silence, go to the theater because that was what Levi liked. She would be able to do the things he liked but not pretend like she liked them too. And he would not leave her for it. Instead, he'd compromise and do things with her that he didn't really like either, just like any normal couple in a healthy relationship.

She would laugh and actually be happy while doing it, instead of just faking her joy. She summoned the images from Levi's social media and merge herself in them, by his side.

Eventually, the images would stop being comforting. They would poke at her heart until it ached, and she would have to brush the pain aside so she wouldn't break down. She would also need to avoid Blaise so he didn't use her fantasy to try and convince her to fall for their imaginary relationship again. She knew she would fall for it if he tried. She always did.

So, Marissa walked out of her room and went to dinner, to find someone, anyone, real to talk to. She avoided the worst cases, people who were stuck in their delusions, and sat next to one of the few people who kept to themselves in silence.

Bethany looked particularly happy today.

"You look chipper."

"My best friend visited me today. That's five times in a row now. My doctor says that she's been helping me avoid Haven." Bethany picked at her food.

"You're still getting visitors?" Marissa felt a pang.

No one had visited her since she admitted herself. She wasn't even sure if anyone knew where she was. If they did, it wasn't like they would care. The company was probably still running without her, ruining the lives of millions in her absence.

But it didn't matter anymore. The world was screwed.

"Her name is Thea. She's a journalist. Maybe I can introduce you to her sometime." Bethany finally took a bite.

Marissa thought the name sounded familiar. She couldn't pin-point exactly why, but it did make her cringe upon hearing it.

"That sounds perfect," Marissa managed to say before leaning back against the metal chair, smiling to herself.

In the end, she did manage to do something extraordinary.

She managed to destroy love forever.

Silver Lining

Silver Lining

Silver Lining

Silver Lining